# THE MORAL MAID'S UNJUST TRIAL

DOROTHY WELLINGS

CORNERSTONETALES.COM

1
EXCITEMENT OF LIFE

LONDON, 1880

"Stay close to me," said Adeline Wenslow, gripping her thirteen-year-old daughter's hand as if her life depended on it. Although Matilda couldn't feel her hand anymore, she obeyed; allowing her mother to drag her through the gruelling streets of London. Women were shouting from windows and laundry was hanging on lines of rope between buildings at multiple heights.

Adeline glimpsed in haste over her shoulder a few times. She'd noticed that a man, who appeared to be under the influence, had been following them through the narrow streets since they left the chapel on Camden Street. Matilda stole a glance and guessed the man might be her dad's age or older.

"We only need to get to Albany Street," Adeline said, panting as she glanced over her shoulder. The drunken man appeared to be distracted by a street seller offering cheap perfumes. They rounded the next corner and Adeline stopped, gasping. She leaned against a cold, moist stone building. The sound of choppy music and drunken laughter flooded the air, identifying it as being an inn or tavern.

"Why did we come this way?" Matilda said, staring at her mother's grim, vexed face. She knew her mother was worried about one of her students, who lived in the safety of the chapel. Parishioners searched for Stephen Canning, a troubled ten-year-old, who went missing two days ago.

"This is the best way to the chapel," said Adeline, now calm and composed. "I take you through only the safest streets, you know that. Are you scared?"

Matilda shook her head.

Adeline stooped and placed a hand over her daughter's shoulder. Pulling her into a firm hug, she said, "I love you." After letting go, she stared into Matilda's dark blue eyes and said with an affectionate smile, "I'll always protect you."

"I know. I love you, too, Mam," said Matilda, who glanced at the looming grey clouds. Can they reach home before the downpour begins? Dad would get worried if they weren't home before him.

Tin cans rolled down a street. Matilda's cheeks stung as the growing force in the air gathered debris. Passers-by bundled up and held onto their hats. The wealthy climbed into their carriages and headed off.

"Let's hurry," Adeline said, rising to her feet. "This weather won't hold for much longer."

Shuffling through narrow, littered streets to Hampstead Road they slipped into Robert Street, which resembled a small alleyway. Matilda was overcome with relief as they headed closer to home. The freezing cobblestones were damp, tiny puddles of water seeped into her shoes and she couldn't feel her toes anymore.

As Adeline opened the front door, a rush of icy wind smacked them.

"Inside quickly," Adeline said, shivering. Once the door was closed, she hurried to the fireplace. "Bring some firewood, would you, Matilda?"

"Yes, Mam," Matilda said and scurried away to the kitchen and found the firewood box. Papa would need to get more. She gathered all she could in her arms and joined her mother at the hearth where she'd kindled a small fire.

Matilda took off her shoes and sat near the fireplace enjoying the cosy sensation of warmth touching her toes and her face. Pressing her hands against her cheeks, they were hot. It would be dark soon; she prayed her father would hurry to get home. She stared around the living room, watching the shadows from the fire lick at their furniture, framed family photographs and the mahogany table—her father inherited it from his father—covered in a crocheted cloth.

The doorknob rattled while Mother was in the kitchen preparing dinner, pots and pans clanging. It wouldn't be long before Mother called her to help. She jumped to her feet and raced to the door as Harold Wenslow slithered between the door and the frame, teeth chattering.

"Oh, hello my dear. You frightened me," said Harold with a light laugh. He leaned over and returned her tight hug. "You're warm. Let me take this wet coat off."

"Mr Wenslow, welcome home," Adeline said, the excitement in her voice evident. She had left the kitchen and greeted her husband with a kiss on his cheek. Her raven hair cascaded from her shoulders and down her back. Matilda loved her mother's hair and hoped hers would be as long when she was an adult.

"Beautiful, as always, Mrs Wenslow," said Harold with a proud smile. He removed his coat and hat, hanging them onto a wall-mounted rack. "It's raining now. Good that you arrived home when you did."

"Uh, when does it stop raining?" Adeline said with a sigh. "Matilda, come help me in the kitchen while your father settles. I'm certain he's had a busy day."

"Yes, Mam," Matilda said.

"Peel the potatoes and carrots. Then set the table."

Matilda answered the same.

Scraping the skin of the potatoes with a knife, Matilda breathed in the scrumptious aroma of beef stew. She cocked her head at the sound of her parents speaking in hushed tones. Whatever it was she was positive they would tell her. They stopped talking. With her father's heavy steps on the creaking timber floor, she imagined him heading to the fireplace to remove his smelly shoes and she giggled.

Matilda dreamed of marrying a wealthy merchant or doctor. Her mother assured her that it was possible. Harold was the supervisor of a prestigious construction company and they had money to afford things others could not.

Until then, she had to be patient. She would be fourteen in the next few weeks and Mam promised she would be old enough to attend the local school. Her mother was a popular teacher and cared for each child as if her own, which is why Stephen's disappearance worried her.

Matilda dropped the knife on the table as her mother glided into the kitchen with a beaming smile.

"Everything all right, Mam?"

"Yes, Stephen has been found," Adeline said with a lilt in her voice. "Your father put the word out and discovered the boy had found work at a construction company. They offered him board and lodgings in exchange for work."

"That's amazing. Do you think he'll become a supervisor like Papa?"

"I don't know. I hope, yes, maybe he will someday..." Adeline said with a smile and scooped her hair into a bun using pins to secure a chignon. "Tomorrow I'll go tell the parishioners at the chapel. Now go set the table; I'll carry on with supper."

With a small nod, Matilda hurried to the dining room, listening to her mother humming from the kitchen. She laid out the glasses, knives, forks and plates in their proper places, ensuring the table—matching the one in the living room—had a dark blue tablecloth. It was her favourite colour.

Adeline declared supper was ready and Matilda helped her bring the food to the table. The three of them sat in their places at the table; Papa at the head, Mam to his right and she sat at Papa's left. They joined hands, as they did every night, and Papa said grace; thanking the Lord for their meal, protection and everlasting love.

∽

SLITHERS OF LIGHT glared into Matilda's eyes, waking her from a deep slumber. Her eyes fluttered open and noticed she hadn't drawn her curtains last night. If Mam knew, she'd be angry. Matilda climbed out of bed and walked to the window, staring through the water-stained glass. Streaks of sun shone between light grey clouds. Towering buildings stood in the way between her window and Regency Park. Standing on her tiptoes and lifting her chin, she could see the green leafy tops peeking at her through the gaps between the buildings. Sometimes Papa and Mam would take her for a picnic and they'd roam around the beautiful garden.

A knock sounded at the door.

"Matilda, are you awake?" It was her mother's voice from behind the door; scraping against the floor as her mother opened it.

"Yes, Mam," she called out from the window, her eyes

drifting over the people going about the start of their day. She stared at her white nightgown, long sleeves with cuffs. "I'll wear my green dress today." She couldn't wear blue again—although she would if she could.

"That's an excellent choice," Adeline said, stretching her neck from around the door. "It's a lovely day; you must wear that matching hat—"

"Uh-no, Mam, please not *that* hat. I don't like the feathers and it's too big. I can't see anything but my feet." She took a breath, heart thumping. She'd never interrupted her mother before. "I'm sure I'll grow into it. Please, I can wear the black bonnet." She gave her mother a pleading stare.

"No, Matilda, the bonnet will not do," Adeline said in a firm voice and entered the room. "You are a young lady and must act and dress like one. Especially if you want to be a teacher one day. You must look the part."

Matilda's heart dropped, but she complied. "I'm sorry. You're right, Mam. I'll wear the green hat. With extra ribbon, it could stay on my head."

"Yes, hurry now. Breakfast is ready."

Matilda remained downcast as she watched her mother leave her room. She walked to the nightstand and lifted the pitcher, pouring water into the small basin. Dabbing a washcloth into the water, she washed her face and wrung out the cloth, leaving it beside the pitcher.

She dressed quickly and without enthusiasm; she found the green hat. Despite its lovely emerald green colour, she loathed its frontal oval shape and long brim, feathers poking from the left side, hugged by a green ribbon band. She ploughed through the drawers of her dressing table and found a green ribbon that would help the hat not slip off her head.

Matilda gazed in the mirror and blinked. She had her mother's sharp features, except for her upturned nose and her curly blond hair, the same as Papa's. She combed her hair until it was straight and secured a neat bun, praying the curly bits wouldn't stick out, but they always did. She complemented her dress with a white pinafore. Mam would help her with the hat.

Satisfied, she left her room and joined her parents for breakfast. Her mother's purple fan-folded dress, narrowing from puffy shoulders to her elbows, was exquisite. Matilda noticed she used a purple ribbon in her braided hair. Why was Mam dressed fancy? Was she going to teach in that dress?

"You look stunning," Harold said, gazing at Matilda. "In a few years, I expect a gentleman to ask for your hand."

Matilda blushed. "Papa, no, you... can't stay things like that."

"Be proud," said Harold, then said with a wink, "Allow your father to dote on his amazing daughter."

"Your father's in a rush eat quickly," Adeline said, prodding Matilda whose plate remained untouched.

Matilda's stomach growled as she eyed the bacon, eggs, cheese and toasted bread. Before her mother could say another word, Matilda devoured her meal and drank a cup of tea that had already been prepared for her.

Harold pushed his chair back, cleared his throat, and rising to his feet said, "I should go."

"Hold on, we'll walk out with you," Adeline said, giving Matilda a loving smile. "There's no school today, so we're going—"

"No school?" Matilda said, her eyes widening. Then why were they dressed up?

"—to have a mother-daughter day," Adeline said with a merry laugh. "I thought we should go to the park."

Papa joined in laughter as he grabbed his coat. "That sounds remarkable. I'd love to join if I could."

"Ladies only," Adeline said and glanced at Matilda as if seeking affirmation.

"What about my hat?" Matilda said with a grimace. While Mother had quickly cleared the table, Matilda had, with reluctance, put the hat on her head and it slipped forward, despite the extra ribbon.

Adeline strode towards Matilda and took the green ribbon from her, and said, "Let's try another way." She tied the ribbon around Matilda's bun, pulled the ribbon forward, behind her ears and ended with a perfect knot beneath Matilda's chin. It still felt wobbly.

"Thank you," Matilda said, looking away from her mother.

A rush of air kissed Matilda's cheek and she saw Papa had the door open. It was time to leave. Mam did say she wanted to visit the chapel. Pushing her thoughts aside, she followed her parents outside, prodding the uncomfortable odd hat on her head.

They walked down the moist narrow street, greeting those they passed, until Hampstead Road. Harold pecked his wife on the cheek and said their goodbyes. Matilda's hat began to slide down the front of her face and the more she pushed it up, the more it came down.

Disoriented and in panic, she left her parent's side. She couldn't see where she was going.

Her palms were clammy and her heart thumped in her head. Was she acting improperly? Would her parents be ashamed of her?

"Matilda!"

It was her mother. She sounded scared. Her father called her name, but not in his usual way. Something was terrifying in his voice.

Hard footfalls and shouting sounded distant as Matilda

pushed the hat back to cover her secure bun. When she looked up, the satisfaction she felt drained from her body.

Matilda was standing in the middle of the road and a horse hitched to a carriage without a driver was cantering towards her. Terror gripped her, and although she willed herself to run, she couldn't; she froze.

The pounding of hooves was deafening mixed with the intense beating of wheels against the cobblestone street and the hollering man running after the carriage.

"Matilda! Run Matilda…" The voices were from Papa and Mam.

"Papa… Mam… help…" Matilda said, barely audible. Tears blurred her vision. Her legs wouldn't move.

The horse grew closer and larger; it had a diamond on its forehead. She could almost taste the horse's vile breath. Without warning, her body jerked sideways, and she landed with a giant 'oof' having the wind knocked from her lungs and she tasted blood in her mouth.

The hollering stopped. The horse's hooves and the carriage wheels had also stopped. Everything stopped. Whimpering, she lifted her aching body and blinked with bewilderment. There was a crowd in the middle of the street where she'd been standing.

"Adeline! My sweet Adeline!" Papa's voice lamented. Dread filled Matilda's heart. One of the men, who witnessed the event, offered his hand to Matilda, helping her on her unsteady feet. The world had stopped, except for her and the stranger helping her stumble toward the crowd.

"What happened?" Matilda stammered. "Where's Papa and Mam?"

The man glanced at the crowd and back at her, and said as if he read her mind, "Don't go there, Miss."

Taking one step at a time, Matilda forced the man to help

her walk the rest of the way to the gathering. Pushing through the crowd, Matilda's blood ran cold at the sight and she dropped to her knees. Crawling to her father, she grasped his arm, staring at her mother lying in his lap; motionless.

"Mam?" Matilda said in a whisper, her voice shaky. "Papa, Mam's going to be all right, won't she?"

Papa appeared defeated. His forlorn expression and red eyes told her what she refused to believe. She shook her head and let go of her father's arm. No, it couldn't be.

Shifting to be near her mother's side, Matilda said, "Wake up, Mam, please wake up."

"Matilda," Papa said in a croaky voice, "She's gone."

"No, no Mam is sleeping," she gently shook her mother as if to prove him wrong, but there was no response.

Tears welled in her eyes and flowed down her cheeks. "Mam, I'm sorry. Please don't die. I promise to be good always, I'll listen to you," Matilda said, her voice breaking. Papa gripped her shoulder, and she looked at him, realising through the grief in his eyes that this was real. Her precious Mam saved her life and was now gone. And it was her fault.

Leaning forward, sandwiched between her parents, Matilda clung to her Mam's lifeless body, sobbing.

2
REMINISCENCE

Papa wasn't his talkative self, he was quiet and a cloud of melancholy oppressed him. Matilda missed him. She was worried but thought it might be the many people coming to pay their respects to her mother. Adeline's friends and parents at the school helped Matilda get her mother ready for the viewing. They didn't have a parlour, so Adeline's coffin rested in the living room. Neither she nor her father went into the living room unless they had to.

Matilda was exhausted from thanking, hugging and shaking strangers' hands over the last three days. Papa looked old and tired. She had to wake him every morning, which was unlike him. He usually was the first one awake.

She sat at the kitchen table drinking a mug of coffee. Her mother never allowed her to drink coffee; it was a scarce luxury for special occasions. Well for this time she was convinced her mother would have allowed an exception due to the circumstances.

The local schoolhouse closed for a week to pay their

respects, but in Matilda's sorrow, she suspected they were only looking for a new teacher. Shivering, she glanced at the red embers fading in the brick stove. After adding firewood and stoking the embers, the flame grabbed the new wood. She did the same for the living room fireplace.

Glimpsing at the coffin, tears welled up in her eyes. Taking one step at a time, Matilda's chest heaved and her heart raced as she approached the coffin. She'd never seen a cadaver until now. Tears slid down her cheeks staring at her mother; beautiful, anyone would think she was sleeping. It reminded her of the story *Snow White* that her mother read to her as a young girl, except her mother didn't have a glass coffin, but a wooden one. There was no poisonous apple, no wicked stepmother and a kiss from Papa would never wake her mother. She was gone.

Footsteps caught her attention and she wiped her eyes. Her father shuffled into the living room and Matilda noticed the dark shadows beneath his bloodshot eyes. His brows furrowed when he saw her and gave her a soulful stare, eyes full of grief and his lips downturned. She'd never seen Papa this way before. His lower lip quivered.

"Matilda," he said in a gravelly voice. He repeated her name took two strides towards her and pulled her into a tight hug. She wrapped her arms around his stomach and listened to him weep. Crushed, Matilda joined him tasting her salty tears.

"I'm ... I'm... sorry, Papa," Matilda said, choking on her words and guilt she'd never experienced before possessed her heart. "It's my fault. If only... I..." her voice strained as her words came out in sobs.

"No, no, it's not your fault," Papa said, squeezing her tight. "I don't blame you. It's... not your... fault." His words were shaky and breathless.

"I'm sorry," he stammered, rising to his feet. "This house,

everything, was your mother's idea. "I don't know what I'm going to do without her." Wiping his eyes, his sniffles and his breaths were shallow.

"Papa, it'll be all right," Matilda said offering a wan smile. Emptiness filled her heart while she stared at her father. She understood his pain and loneliness. Nothing would be the same again. She and her father would survive. That is what Mam would want, for them to keep going. Tears pricked the back of her eyes and she blinked them back. She needed to be strong for Papa.

A thump at the door caught Papa's attention and with slumped shoulders, he ambled towards the door.

It was Pastor Donald Harris from the chapel in Camden Town. He stood at the door, dressed in black with a solemn expression. Matilda watched them shake hands.

"I'm sorry for your loss. Mrs Wenslow's kindness will never be forgotten. Her contribution to helping the needy... we are eternally grateful." The pastor's baritone voice held sympathy. "Forgive my intrusion I want to finalise the funeral arrangements. I hope this is not an inconvenient time?"

"Go to the kitchen, Matilda," Papa said extending his hand to the pastor and bidding him towards the living room. "You'll have tea, won't you?"

The pastor nodded with a courteous smile and followed Papa towards the living room.

Matilda exhaled a silent sigh. She knew they would be talking about unpleasant matters and that her father wanted to protect her from the evils of the world, but what could be worse than witnessing and being responsible for her mother's death?

She heard the men talk while she set a pot on the brick stove to boil water. Because Mam died in a tragic accident she could be buried in the church's cemetery. Papa didn't want to talk about it, but the pastor was persistent; in a calm manner.

By the time Matilda had brewed the tea and set out the tray, the pastor had won the battle and Papa consented by thanking him for the kind gesture. The patrons of the chapel will organise flowers and the cold, hard funeral music that she'd heard at her grandfather's funeral three years ago. Papa began to weep again, but he held back his tears when she walked into the room balancing the tray so the liquid did not spill out of the cups.

Matilda left the room and returned to the kitchen where a third cup of tea was waiting for her. Her heart shattered at her Papa's wails and she heard the pastor's compassionate encouragement.

"How can… I be a good father? I go to work…" his words jumbled, but the pastor understood them.

"She loves you and is hurting, too. Help her understand that accidents happen. There is no reason for them. There is no way to know when they will happen."

"She blames herself, but… that blasted hat. Matilda didn't want to wear it."

"Hat or not. We can't understand the Lord's ways. He has a purpose for our lives in ways we'll never understand."

"It's not that I don't believe, Pastor Harris, I just… I don't know how I can be strong for me, much less Matilda." His voice broke into unrelenting sobs.

More mumbling and jumbled words. She sipped her piping hot tea, tasting its sweetness and licked her lips. Papa was a good father, what did he mean? She decided to be strong for both of them. Mam told her once that everyone needed help at times in their lives and it was our duty to help them. Maybe this was what Mam meant. It was her time to help her father.

Matilda gave a sad smile, imagining her mother sitting opposite her with a mug of tea, sharing biscuits, while waiting for Papa to come home.

"I'll help, Papa, Mam. I promise," Matilda whispered and sipped her tea.

3
MOVING ON

EIGHTEEN MONTHS LATER

Matilda jiggled the front door handle as if it were a game of tug-of-war. Clutching the bags of groceries in her arms, she cringed as she pushed the door, its slanted edge scraping against the battered floor and hinges whining like a hungry baby. The back of her neck was moist and she hurried to get inside and out of the unbearable heat.

She breathed in stale air which held a heated scent; a mix of damp cotton mustiness, something powerfully sweet and sour. She gagged almost dropping the bags, and hurried to the kitchen. Placing them on the kitchen table, she opened every window that had been closed from the deadly wind the night before.

Despite the uncontrollable heat, Matilda opened the kitchen door and welcomed in fresh air. Her nostrils flared as she drew in a deep breath. Regaining her poised state, she gazed at the kitchen and with frustration blew air through her lips.

She'd been feeling ill for the past few days and retired to bed early not realising that it gave her father a chance to find an open tavern. Papa was home and as she expected when she walked into the living room, he was sprawled across the two-seater couch surrounded by bottles of whiskey and unfamiliar liquor.

Tip-toeing towards him, she lifted her chin and sniffed, recoiling at the sour and musty odour from his clothes. She glanced at him with pity and sadness watching his chest rise and fall, his malty breath evident as he snorted like piglets in a barnyard.

Matilda imagined his full face and glowing cheeks above a bright smile, which was now haggard and gaunt. She couldn't remember when he last shaved or cut his hair, sticky and caked with whatever had been slopped on him.

Taking care to not disturb him, Matilda picked up the bottles, five in total. Did he drink all this alone? Who would sell him this many bottles of alcohol?

Whenever she offered to help him, he'd get angry and defensive. While he sat drinking and frolicking between taverns, wearing the same clothes for days, she sat at home worrying about him. She had lost her mother; she didn't want to lose her father, too.

"Oh, Papa," Matilda said, the corners of her eyes drooping and her chest flooded with pain. She wished he knew how much she missed him. She took one last look at him before heading to the kitchen. She assumed a friend or fellow patron must've helped him home. When she left early to buy groceries she had thought he was sleeping in late like he frequently did. She was oblivious to the possibility of him becoming intoxicated.

What would Mam think of him acting this way? Whenever

Matilda pointed it out, he became upset and would storm out in a rage.

As she packed away the groceries, she smiled anticipating the joy on Papa's face when he tasted her apple pie. She heard him grumble from the living room and her heart felt like it had split in two.

"Ade... lines... my Ade..."

Matilda swiped the tears that brimmed in her eyes. If only Mam had survived. Papa wouldn't be like this and their lives would be normal—the way it was before. Shoving his words and her thoughts aside, she set the hearth alight and fried eggs, bacon, and toasted bread—the way Mam taught her—adding a pot of water for tea.

There was a solid knock at the door. Matilda wiped her hands on a cloth and rushed to the front door to answer. A harder, impatient knock sounded.

"Just a minute," Matilda said, raising her voice, but not enough to wake Papa. She jiggled the door handle and her cheeks grew red at the grinding sound until the door was partially opened.

A young man with beady eyes stared at her and remained silent, his pose like a soldier.

"May I help you?"

"Yes, ma'am. Is this the residence of a man named Harold Wenslow?"

Matilda's head bobbed. "Yes, he's my father. He can't see you right now, because..." her mind raced. She couldn't tell this strange man the truth. "He's resting now. Hasn't been himself lately."

The man's arm extended, and in his hand, he held out an envelope. "It's official, ma'am, I'm sorry. Mr Wenslow hasn't been at work for a week," Matilda gasped with her head inclined, listening. The man continued, "Except for that time he came to work drunk and we sent him home, but one of our workers saw him at Lucky Horse later that day."

Holding her breath, Matilda took the envelope from him and exhaled. She tried to calm her staggered breathing. Stunned and appalled to hear the man's words. An invisible bolt of lightning shot through her body. Whatever was inside this envelope couldn't be good. The only letters they received were unpaid bills.

"What does the letter say?" she probed, fingering the corners of the envelope. Her mouth went dry.

"I'm not supposed to say ma'am, but Mr Wenslow has been demoted. He must return to work tomorrow or he'll be without employment." The young man leaned forward and added, "These days it is best to not be without employment." His mouth was set in a grim line and he nodded with a dramatically arched brow. "That is all. Have a good day, ma'am," he said, tipping his hat. He turned on his heels, leaving Matilda stunned, gaping at his lanky frame.

She glanced at the letter before closing the door. Her pounding heart raced faster as she opened the envelope signed by the manager, Peter Benson; it was as the young man had said. Had Papa spent all the money at taverns and pubs?

Matilda clenched the letter in her hand. Her father's job was on the line and here he was in the living room recovering from those empty bottles she'd discarded. She heard Papa stir in the living room. The couch sang and the floor creaked. Marching into the living room, she thrust the letter onto his lap. His eyes squinted, his face full of confusion and dried spittle pasted his hair to his mouth.

"What is this, Papa?" said Matilda, anger brewing from the pit of her stomach. This was likely why they continued to receive letters of unpaid bills and short of rent. Her father was drinking the money away instead of paying the bills.

With the letter in his hands, he stared at it as if he'd never seen one before.

"What's this?" he mumbled. He rubbed his forehead with his left hand. "Too much light," he said and lay down, releasing the letter with his right hand. It floated to the floor like a leaf ignored by the current of the wind.

"Papa read it," Matilda insisted. She scooped the letter from the floor and shoved it into his face. "You spend all your time at the taverns. What about our bills? If you don't go back to work, they'll fire you."

He groaned and sat up. "What are you talking about?" he said, his voice rough, and he pushed the mop of hair from his face. "We're fine. There's nothing to worry about."

While he read the letter, she sat beside him and said, "Papa, you can't go on like this. You won't get the same pay as before. I read the letter. They have appointed a new supervisor."

Harold slumped onto the couch, gazing at the ceiling with a defeated expression.

"You're right, Matilda," he said and looked at her with sorrow in his eyes, reaching for her hand. "I will try harder, I promise. I'll speak to the manager. He'll give me another chance." Harold buried his face in his hands, rubbing his forehead with the tips of his fingers. "I'll get a shave and haircut and go speak to Mr Benson."

Matilda wrapped her arms around her father and said, "Papa, yes, please do that. At least then you can keep your job."

He nodded with the best smile he could muster, but Matilda recognised the unhappiness behind it. She learnt how to hide her pain from him. If he couldn't handle his own, how could he help with her grief?

While he washed up and changed his clothes, Matilda brewed the tea and set breakfast on the kitchen table. Since

Mam had passed away, they seldom ate in the dining room. Her empty seat was haunting.

Papa looked neat as a pin when he returned and devoured his breakfast before heading out, giving Matilda a confident wave.

Closing her eyes, Matilda prayed Mr Benson would listen and take pity on her father.

4
THE MOVE

Matilda peeked through the curtain facing the street. Sunset had begun and Papa was not home yet. Her heart palpitated. What if something terrible happened to Papa? She lost Mam, she could not lose Papa. Then she'd be alone.

She stared at the soft pinks, purples, blues and the disappearing yellow-orange in the sky, hoping Papa would appear. The heaviness that grew in her heart was unbearable. If Papa was not home by now, Matilda knew if she walked into the closest tavern there, he would be.

Walking to the living room, she sank into the couch and stared at the embers that glowed an intense red. Excruciating pain rushed into her chest and it took sheer willpower to not shriek in anguish. She covered her face with the palms of her hands and bawled. Her heart squeezed with agony recalling the happy times with Papa. As a young girl, they'd go to the park and, much to Mam's objections; he'd carry her on his shoulders running around the lake. How could she get through to him? She wanted her Papa back.

At the sound of staggered bangs on the door, she stopped crying and grabbed her handkerchief. Dabbing her eyes and face, she gathered the confidence to appear normal. She opened the door and a man—her father—tumbled inside, groaning. Two bulky men glared down at her.

"I-I'll scream if you try to hurt me," Matilda said, a strange sensation from the pit of her stomach overflowed her body with strength. "Don't come any closer."

"This man live 'ere," the bulky muscular man asked in a cockney accent.

"Yes, he's my father."

"He ain't welcome at Blue Joe's," the dark-haired mass of muscle said. "We won't go easy on 'im, if we see him. He causes trouble with the patrons. You tell him, yeah?"

Matilda swallowed, clutching the folds of her fanned front dress, and nodded. "Yes, I'll be sure to tell him. I'm sorry for the trouble."

The men tipped their hats with a small nod and walked away.

Matilda didn't realise she was holding her breath until she exhaled. Her heart thumped against her chest as adrenaline rushed through her veins. Closing the door with force, she glanced at her father squirming on the floor, groaning.

"Papa, what happened?" She stared at his black-and-blue face, purple swelling at the corner of his left eye. She jumped to her feet, after noticing dried blood on his lips and face. Grabbing a cloth, she soaked it in a bowl of cool water and returned to her father.

Dabbing the cool cloth against his lips, cheeks and eyes, Harold whined. She cleaned the dried blood and repeated her actions until his face was clean.

"So-ory, uh…" his malty voice said. "Wasn'… my… faul…i…"

"Papa, stop talking. You're not making sense," said Matilda, squeezing the cloth inside the bowl of water. "Rest on the couch and tell me tomorrow what happened."

"I have my job..." Harold hiccupped, "Mr Benson told me off. Gave me a piece of his mind, he said to me that... I was lucky..."

"Stop Papa," Matilda said, warm liquid pricked at the back of her eyes. How many nights must this go on?

"...he's letting me stay because he... likes you. Nice girl, he said... giving me," he belched, "another chance... matrimony maybe..."

"You don't know what you're saying," Matilda said, disregarding his last words. With a grunt and drawing in a deep breath, Matilda helped her father to the couch.

"Hold the cloth to your eye, Papa," said Matilda. She rushed to the kitchen and grabbed a glass of water and a beef sausage, which was now cold. She'd prepared mashed potatoes, vegetables and freshly baked bread to cheer him up.

She joined her father in the living room and helped him drink and forced him to eat.

"It will help sober you up," Matilda said, unconvinced. Rumours she'd heard in town from random talk.

"There's more I must tell you," Harold said, averting his eyes. "Are there more sausages?"

Matilda stood to her feet, ignoring the aches and pains in her muscles and joints. As her father requested, she brought him his portion of supper. She'd placed a pot of water onto the stove positive tea would help him sober up.

"How much worse can it become?" Matilda said, watching him, without utensils, eat his sausages and dab them in the mash.

"Well, I need to tell you something. I got a letter from the landlord and he says by letter of the court we must leave this house," he paused, taking a sip of water. "The rent is overdue and my pay is less," he sighed with a dejected look in his eyes. "We can't afford to stay here. I've no excuse and I'm sorry." Red-eyed he briefly glanced at the ceiling. "I spoke to a friend, my manager, at the construction company. He owns a small two-bedroom house and he says we can stay there."

"Stay where?" Matilda said. A sinking feeling twirled in her stomach as she left to prepare the tea. What friend was Papa talking about? One time he took her with him to work and explained that the men kept to themselves except for lunch times. She stopped between the doorframe and half turned to look at him.

"Where is the house?"

Harold's shoulders slumped forward and hung his head in his hands before gazing at her. "I'm sorry. The house is in Whitechapel." Shame cast a shadow on him. "There's nowhere else to go. He is charging us half the rent than anywhere else."

Whitechapel. It was at the east end of London and one of the worst slums, full of unsavoury characters, high crime and notorious for its lack of sanitation. She offered a grateful smile at him. "It's all right, Papa, I know you're doing your best. I was thinking about finding a place to work. It would help us, wouldn't it? We need the money."

"No, no, there'll be enough." He said waving his arm in the air. "It won't be the same, not what we're used to, but we'll manage."

"When do we leave?"

"Tomorrow," he whispered, eyes drooping. Laying his head back against the soft upholstery, mouth open wide, he fell into a deep sleep. Snoring in peace, leaving Matilda alone to start packing.

THE TASTE of ash and dirt stuck on Matilda's tongue. Papa pulled the lead tied to a donkey that was hitched to an old wagon—cheap hire from the livery—carrying less than half of what they owned. Papa decided to sell anything they couldn't take with them. As she and Papa trundled along the streets of Whitechapel towards Adler Street, she glanced at the soggy garbage lining the streets stuck to the corners of the pavement; open sewers and puddles of stale water permeated the air.

Despite the sun beaming alongside distant grey clouds the mould-infested buildings were gloomy and miserable. People yelling and shrieking from stalls and shady-looking businesses fared their chance for a quid from Papa, who shook his head.

People mulling about the flower shops, grocers, clothing stores, inns, blacksmiths and more. Matilda never dreamed there were this many businesses this side of London. She'd only heard terrible stories and now she and her father were going to be staying in the slums of those stories under the noses of some of the most wealthy, affluent people in London.

Matilda gazed at her father, who had noticed the many taverns. Some were crowded; others were like an empty tinderbox. She prayed in her heart that her father's promises of turning over a new leaf would ring true. They had a roof over their heads and if Papa stopped visiting the taverns, they could land back on their feet again.

"Why don't you sit on the donkey?" Harold said, catching her eye. "You are looking drained and sleepy."

He didn't look much better, but she didn't tell him that. Instead, she offered a brave, reassuring smile that she did not feel.

"I'm fine, Papa," she said with mustered-up fake courage. "The poor animal wasn't the strongest in the livery and I think it can't handle any more weight."

"Yes, right." Harold's eyes fell upon the donkey and he commented, "The animal does look sickly."

The livery owner called the donkey, Albert, named after his ex-father-in-law. Neither Matilda nor Harold encouraged him to share the story behind Albert—just Albert, no surname.

"I can walk the rest of the way. It can't be too much farther, can it?"

With a slight shake of his head, Harold answered, "No, just past two more streets. There will be rows of houses."

Matilda remembered walking through the streets of London with Mam and being enamoured by the beauty of the magnificent mansions. With one turn they found clumped buildings lined in rows like tightly squeezed lemons for fresh lemonade.

Her throat was dry and by the time they found Adler Street. It was no different from the ones they'd passed by. She and Papa shared a look of uncertainty.

"Our new home," Harold said.

She saw the misery behind his enthusiastic smile, arms outstretched and his open palms facing the haggard building numbered twenty-nine. A soft sigh escaped her lips as she stared at her grim home with only one window in the front glaring down at her. She noticed in the middle of Adler Street there was a water pump and a few outhouses.

"Our new home," she repeated, attempting to return his smile, but her heart ached for her mother. And with tears in her eyes, she whispered into the air, "I miss you, Mam."

Harold opened the door and waved his hand in the air. "Get inside and have a look. I'll begin unpacking. You can choose which room you'd like."

Matilda walked toward the door and hastily stepped aside as a half-dressed young boy careened in her direction chasing what appeared to be a ball. A group of boys clamouring to get ahead rushed past her following the first boy. Their bare feet slushed into the puddles of water.

She imagined the students her mother had taught. They wore respectable clothes and didn't behave in such a manner. This was a world unfamiliar to her, but she was confident that they wouldn't live in this place for long. She climbed two small steps before entering a short, narrow tunnel. Everything was dark and she noticed the lack of light as she squinted her eyes. Where were the windows?

The air was moist with an earthy scent and the walls were damp to the touch. Her eyes adjusted to the dark and she noted the kitchen and living room were separated by thin boards of timber. A staircase hugging the wall, which she guessed led to the bedrooms. The staircase groaned as she walked upstairs. A ridiculously small passage led to two bedrooms each the size of her mother's pantry. There were rusted cots with stained mattresses in each room. She was relieved they'd brought sheets and blankets.

Scuffling sounded at the door and Matilda heard her father panting. She hurried down the stairs and found him leaning against the door with two large bags on the floor. Matilda covered her mouth with a giggle, they were her bags and she had no trouble carrying either of them.

"What do you think?" Harold said with furrowed brows. "I haven't seen it. This is the first time."

Matilda held her breath, exhaled and said, "There's nothing that a good painting or photograph can't do on the wall. We can put up Mam's pictures on the wall, can't we? What about the paintings she loved?"

Harold grinned and stared at her with relief. "Yes, I like that. Let's make this place our home."

5
AN OBSTACLE

ONE YEAR LATER

Matilda walked from the water pump carrying two buckets of water. Breathless after five steps, she withheld the strain on her muscles until she reached her front door. When she first began fetching water, she'd make multiple stops to catch her breath. She had to learn to keep going and endure the pain otherwise she would gain attraction from the wrong crowd of people.

Her heart melted at the amount of people, including children and old people, who lived on the streets and alleyways. All in search of warmth or a few pennies. If their house was bigger she was certain that her father wouldn't mind having an additional occupant. The extra company would be welcomed.

Rubbing her deep pink and aching hands, she hoped her father would come home early. Four months after moving onto Adler Street, her father ventured into various pubs: Brown Bear, Royal Oak and more. He spent more nights at the pub than at home and when he did arrive; he was beyond reason or of sound mind. Picking up the buckets sloshing water over the sides, she walked inside the house with a hopeful heart.

She poured the buckets of water inside a medium-sized barrel. Her father would need to get more. Her body was stiff and her muscles ached. Shivering, she grabbed a shawl and wrapped it around her shoulders. The tiny cast iron stove was of little help due to the cracks in the walls and moisture. There was a smaller, inoperable window at the back of the house and both window sills were damaged, allowing the cutting flow of air to drift inside.

Matilda added coal into the stove hoping it wasn't damp from the moisture in the air. After a few tries and a couple of sparks, a small flame appeared. Satisfied the fire wouldn't go out, she ran her hands over dangling clothing which hung over a rope her father had tied inside their house. They were still damp, but the heat from the fire would dry them.

She grabbed onions, potatoes and vegetables. Tonight they'd have soup. Matilda always checked the stained window at the back of the house when the afternoon turned darker. She'd see her father walking along Whitechapel Street, but lately this seldom happened. She checked and he was not there.

Placing the heavy lid over the top of the pot, she headed upstairs to her room. She glanced at an old photograph hanging on the dire wall. It was of her, Mam and Papa standing close together and her heart clenched with anguish. She'd give anything to go back to the way things were. The room had no windows and she missed the view from her old bedroom window and watching the sun lower behind the park trees. Closing her eyes, she imagined the vivid colours exploding and running wild in the sky.

Why did Mam have to die? Although Papa told her numerous times it wasn't her fault, guilt raked her.

Thumping sounded at the door, which startled her. Did she miss seeing her father walk down the wide-ranging street? She hurried downstairs, listening to the continuous banging on the door. Swinging the door open, her eyes widened. It was a Bobby with a grim frown on his face.

SHE GREETED him noticing his posh tunic with a single row of shiny silver buttons down his slim front torso and on his head a high bowl-shaped hat. "How can I help you, officer?"

"Miss Matilda Wenslow?" He said in a curt voice.

"Yes, I am she," Matilda's pulse increased gradually. She could only assume it was regarding her father.

"Constable Hamish at your service. I'm sorry to trouble you at this hour," he said with a thick British accent and adjusted his well-fitted hat. "Your father, Mr Harold Wenslow... he is your father, isn't he?"

Matilda nodded, and a sick sensation engulfed her body. "I'm waiting for him. Has something happened?"

The bobby huffed, "Has something happened, indeed," he tutted, "Your father has been charged with murder and you're next of kin. This is the purpose of my visit. To inform you."

Matilda gaped at him. "No, there must be a mistake. My father could never ki-kill anyone." The words barely escaped her lips. "He'd never... He'd never hurt a fly."

"I assure you, Miss Wenslow, he was involved in a quarrel with other patrons. It was quite the collie shangies, I believe. The suspect, uh, your father, in a drunken rage, pushed another patron, a diplomat—I might add—down some stairs," he cocked a thick brow, "All drunk and mad as hatters. Need I say the diplomat did not make it he died instantly according to the doctor. It does not look promising for Mr Wenslow."

All hope drained from her. Murder, her father being accused of murder was foolishness. It couldn't be true.

"When can I see him?" Matilda said, her brows furrowed staring at the bobby, who was unaware of the rush of impending waves of terror shooting through her veins.

"I'll escort you, Miss Wenslow," he said, pulling at his tunic. "There is a carriage waiting to transport you to the police station."

"All right, let me grab my coat," Matilda said, throwing the shawl from her shoulders and raced upstairs to her room. It wasn't a grand coat, but it warmed her over chilly nights. She shrugged into the black-striped coat and hurried to join the police officer.

Feeling the suspicious scowls and stares, Matilda kept her head down as she followed the bobby to the carriage. She couldn't climb inside fast enough and could only imagine what their neighbours were thinking. Whitechapel was a large community, but when it came to rumours it became a small place.

Matilda stared out the window watching the sky darken, absent of colour. The gas street lamps were flickering casting shadows over the filth and vermin-infested streets. The carriage jolted forward and the driver hollered something incoherent, Constable Hamish appeared to understand and hollered back. Within minutes, the carriage wheels crushed the dirt and grit beneath them.

∽

LEMAN STREET POLICE Station was as depressing as the rows of buildings on Whitechapel Street. Above the entrance were four enormous double-paned windows set in brick and overlooked a bricked archway with one double-paned window on either side. Street lamps lit up the pavement and Matilda climbed the two stone steps and strode into the police station.

"Where's my father?" Matilda said, perusing the police station. There was a polished wooden counter with two bobbies dressed in the same attire as Constable Hamish, except at the edge of their sleeves were two horizontal stripes. Against the wall on Matilda's left were two empty benches. Voices sounded through a passage that was blocked by a locked massive steel gate.

"He's in the cell, of course," Constable Hamish said, giving her a shake of his head implying her question was senseless. "You'll see him. Can't take him home, he needs to stand trial. In front of the judge at the courthouse."

The constable grabbed a bunch of keys from one of the bobbies at the counter and pushed it inside the keyhole of the gate. She heard the click as the key turned and the hinges squeaked as he opened it.

Pointing a white-gloved hand at her, Constable Hamish said, "Don't get any ideas now. The keys are kept at the counter and not with me. There are two other criminals in there—"

"My father's not a criminal," Matilda's voice rose in anger. How dare this man call her father a criminal? He knew nothing of her father and his troubles.

"—just ignore them, don't talk to them. Mr Wenslow is in the third cell. Stay seated on the bench."

Furious at the way Constable Hamish disregarded her, she glared at him and said nothing. It would do nothing to scream at the police officer and be arrested, too.

"Thank you," Matilda said, her hands balled at her sides, clutching her soft coat. Her father would explain everything and the police would have no choice, but to let him go.

"Go on, then," the constable said, holding the gate steady. "I'm not going to hold this gate open all night for you."

Matilda glared at him with suspicion and a sigh of frustration blew from his mouth.

"I'm not going to keep you in there. I go off shift soon and you only have thirty," he lifted his left wrist, "oh no, twenty-five minutes to talk to your father so I suggest you get in there and talk to him."

Without rebuttal, Matilda shot him a dark look and walked through the gate overhearing the constable remark to a fellow officer, "Maybe get a confession out of him."

"Yeah?" the other officer responded. "We have what we need, but maybe we keep her, a secretary here won't be a bad thing, right?"

They chortled and she kept walking.

The prison cells were cold. She counted four cells in total. The man in the first cell was lying on a rusted, banged-up cot, holding his stomach and groaning. She noticed the chamber pot and there was nothing else. The second cell was the same and the prisoner banged his hands against the steel bars, cussing at her with crude remarks as she passed by.

Her only concern was her father, who was sitting on the cot that was less rusty than the one in the first cell. He glanced at her and shot to his feet. Both raced towards the bars and clutched their hands through the gaps.

"I didn't think you'd come," Harold said. "The police said they told you the truth. Their version, that is, I didn't do this. You believe me, don't you?" His eyes were searching her face and she knew he wanted an affable answer. Besides his whiskey breath, he was sober and appeared clean and unharmed. His clothes were scruffy.

"I-I want to believe you. I thought you were in a fight," Matilda said, relief flooding through her veins. She had imagined the worst. A black, swollen eye, bloodied face, cuts on his body or broken ribs. She pushed her thoughts aside. "What happened, Papa?"

He bit on his top lip and his eyes trailed to the timber floor. He gave a half-shrug and said, "I'm not sure. I was at the Black Oak tavern having a drink at the bar." His head whipped up and his eyes were desperate. "I swear I didn't have much to drink. I was not drunk. The tavern was quiet, not many people, just three others and they got into a fight. A mean one. It started getting bad and I paid for my drink, I didn't finish it and got up to leave." He paused and tears came to his eyes, her heart pulsated when she heard him whisper, "Oh, Adeline."

"Papa, what happened next? The bobbies are saying you are going to be on trial for murder."

"You don't believe me, either," he said in a soft tone. He gripped the bars and glared at his daughter. "I didn't do this. I am innocent. You know me."

"Papa, I don't have much time. Tell me everything you remember. I'll find a barrister or someone who can help you."

Harold gazed at her and she'd never seen him in utter despair. "I turned to leave and the one man saw me. He didn't like me leaving the drink so I told him he could have it if he wanted. The man couldn't walk straight and nothing he said made sense." He ran his hands through his hair.

"I never raised my voice. I didn't threaten anyone. The other two men kept away from him and seemed scared. If I wasn't blocking the door, I would have seen the fourth man. He was hiding away in a corner on his own. Didn't say much, just got up and pushed the drunken man outside. They threw punches at each other. Me and the other two tried to stop it..."

He exhaled a calm breath staring at the ceiling. "The tavern owner was chasing everybody out anyway. The next thing I knew there was screaming and shouting for help. I ran over and saw the man had fallen down some stairs that lead to a downtown alleyway." Tears slipped down her father's cheeks and he stared at her. "The man died, I saw it. His neck was broken from the fall. The only way... only way he could have fallen is if... Matilda someone pushed that man. And it *wasn't* me."

Matilda was quiet as she sat on the floor. She didn't know what to think. Her father had never lied to her, why would he start now? But the police were confident they had all the evidence they needed. Her father had broken his promises about going to the taverns and pubs.

Anger and hatred brewed in her heart. She wanted to scream at him. That he was a liar. Anyone drunk enough can hurt another person. If only he avoided going to those places, he would not be in this situation.

"Papa, why didn't you come home?"

"You're right. I should have, but I had a bad day at work and I needed something to take the edge off. I only had two glasses of whisky, nothing else."

Guilt replaced the anger in her heart. She knew her father better than anyone. Drunk or not, he could never hurt another person. He seldom got angry and he was not a violent person. There had to be a way to prove his innocence.

"I believe you," Matilda reached for the bars again to hold his hand. Through the corner of her eye, she noticed the police on duty weren't paying much attention to her. "Is that everything? Could you identify the other man?"

Harold shook his head, "That's all I remember. I was knocked to the ground and then the bobbies picked me up telling me what I'd done. I tried to tell them the truth, but they wouldn't hear any of it."

Deafening banging against steel resonated down the

passage and a male voice yelled, "Hurry up in there. You have five minutes and if you're not out, I'll drag you out."

Matilda's eyes widened in horror. Was this all the time she had with her father? The police didn't tell her when the trial would happen.

"When is the trial?"

"I think in three days," Harold said with a half-hearted shrug and slumped against the wall separating him from the vacant cell. "I've heard the police talking. They're saying some rich diplomat was killed and they need to blame someone. I happened to be in the wrong place at the wrong time. Living in Whitechapel doesn't help either."

"I know, Papa," Matilda said, giving her father a comforting smile. "I'll think of something. You and Mam still have friends that can help."

"No, you can't approach them," Harold said, viewing her from his seated position. He shifted closer and wrapped his fingers over hers, still clutching the bars. "I don't know who's involved, but there's a conspiracy. I'm being framed for someone else. You know how it goes. Someone rich does something, the bobbies and the judge get paid off... there's nothing we can do."

A cloud of sadness fell between them and the pain of injustice grew in her heart.

"It's not fair," Matilda said. Her father's hand was damp from his tears and she inhaled to keep her emotions calm. She promised Mam that she'd be strong for them both. "There must be a way, Papa, I'll talk to the police again and tell them to investigate."

Her father gave a wan smile. Despite the sorrow on his face, in his eyes, she detected the love he had for her. "I'm sorry, Matilda. I haven't been a good father. I've done nothing but make you worry. Please forgive me."

"I forgave you long ago, Papa," she said with another smile and pressed her forehead against his, ignoring the icy steel bars.

The click of the gate sounded and they instantly pulled away. Heavy-heeled boots thumped on the floor.

"I'll visit you again," Matilda said, backing towards the bench where she was told to sit, "It's a promise."

By the time the police officer arrived, a sergeant, who had reddish hair curling from the edges of the high custodian helmet. He held a black stick in his hand.

"Time to go," the man said, his voice kinder than Constable Hamish. "The horseman is waiting for you. Go on home and rest. You'll be told when the trial happens."

"I love you, Papa," Matilda said sniffling. "I'll see you soon."

Harold bit on his upper lip and he nodded, mouthing *I love you, too.*

Wiping her eyes, she followed the sergeant walking further and further away from her father. In silence, Matilda obeyed the sergeant's instructions, but she couldn't remember anything more he said. Heartbroken, all she could think about was her father stuck in that miserable cell.

She was alone inside the carriage. At the jolt of movement mixed with the sound of the carriage wheels, her heart exploded and she sobbed like she'd never done before.

6

PREJUDICED TRIAL

It was not easy to get inside the Justice Hall from Old Bailey Street; otherwise also known as Old Bailey or Central Criminal Court. The stone and brick walls were filled to the brim, any more guests would burst into the adjoining Newgate Prison. The diplomat's death proved to be quite the scandal within the longest three days of Matilda's life. The affluent were privy to pay money as if going to the theatre and her father was the main actor.

The addition of a the fourth courtroom, limited seating for the public, there was no space for anyone from the middle class or lower to attend. People huddled near the stained windows hoping to find a place where if they they could not view the proceedings, they might hear something of it.

"I need to go inside," said Matilda hedging her way past a bobby, who stared at her with a menacing look in his eyes.

"Git out of here," the bobby demanded lifting his stick trying to push back the sea of people. His plump cheeks stretched across his face thinning his line moustache. "Show me your ticket. You don't have a ticket, do you?"

"It's my father's trial," she said taking a small breath and holding back her tumultuous emotions. "I need to be with him."

She wore her best dark blue dress. Why wouldn't he let her inside? She was clean, and respectable and had found her white gloves and matching shoes. Her attire had seen better days, but she ensured her appearance was as her Mam had taught her. Closing her eyes, Matilda remembered her mother's words, *'if you want to be a teacher, you must look the part* right now, she knew she looked the part to get inside Justice Hall.

"Yeah? That's what everybody's saying," the bobby said, his voice holding a mix of frustration and annoyance. He puffed out his chest staring down at her from the top step.

She glanced at his uniform and noticed his sleeve had no stripes.

"You know Constable Hamish, don't you?" Matilda said, fingers crossed, she knew this rabbit-out-the-hat trick may not work.

"Huh? Hamish?" the bobby nodded, his brows furrowed. "The constable from Leman Police Station?"

"Yes!" Matilda stated with excitement, trying to keep her composure. "He'll vouch for me. He was there... he was the one who arrested my father. I went to the station and there were two sergeants, but I don't know their names."

"Shame for you, huh?" he said, mouth curving into a smile. "I know many constables—"

Matilda's heart sank. Was she going to miss her father's trial? Tears pricked at her eyes. Her one last chance at being with her father and supporting him was blocked by a brawny bobby.

"—don't look like that," the bobby sighed with a roll of his eyes and he scoffed, "Yeah, I do know him. Don't like him, though. Maybe it's his gibface or something. Acts high and mighty, the foozler. It's no wonder he's still a constable."

Peering at her, he continued. "You look like a sweet lady, Tell you what. I'll let you in," he said with a gleam in his eyes and Matilda's heart surged with hope.

"You've dressed nice, but I can see you ain't got a ticket and not one of them rich folks," he said rubbing his smooth chin and a proud smile crinkled his cheeks. He pointed a thick forefinger at his chest. "If you see him, you tell him I let you inside. Constable Arbott. Remember my name, yeah?"

He appeared a few years younger than Hamish. Why had he not stepped up from being a constable? She wasn't going to ask him.

"Constable Arbott," Matilda repeated. "Yes, I'll be sure to tell him. So you'll let me through?"

"Git inside then," he said, jerking his head in the direction of the entrance with a smile that could bring on summer. "It's courtroom one, I think."

Matilda thanked him and rushed inside before he could change his mind. She squeezed past the tight crowds and made her way to courtroom one. Her eyes widened staring at the vast U-shaped auditorium. It was as though she was to attend a pantomime.

She noticed the two wooden stalls on either side of the room that were for the jury—as her barrister had explained when they met—and her father would stand in a wooden landing with a railing called a dock that was raised in the centre of the room. Below the dock were tables for the prosecutor, barrister and solicitors. Between the judges and the court officials was the witness box. At the head of the room was a platform raised higher than the stalls and dock where the judges were already getting themselves seated.

High balconies on both sides of the room were brimming

with individuals exerting the scent of prestige and fortune churning Matilda's stomach. Even from where she stood, Matilda heard the creaking and whining as the onlookers shifted in the balconies.

Matilda hurried down the stairs attempting to ignore the stares as she made her way to join the barrister, George Webber. He graduated from law school two years ago and as a childhood friend, George agreed to help her father because he, too, believed Harold was innocent. At five years old George's father went missing—only to reappear ten years later—it was Harold who had picked up the pieces and took on a fatherly role. This inspired George to become a solicitor because he wanted to protect the innocent just as he felt Harold had protected him.

"Good, you're here," George said in his deep, formal, professional voice. Matilda would tease him about it, but not today.

"Yes, thank you, but only in the nick of time. The bobby wasn't going to let me inside. I thought if he knew that horrible constable who arrested my father, he'd let me in. Well, he did, but not for the reasons I thought."

George ran his hand over his wig that covered his head, the curling into rolls dangling at his cheeks and straightened his sharp black gown, which was pleated at the shoulders. Matilda perused the stalls, all the court officials wore similar attire. The higher the position, the more stately and glamorous the attire.

"Take your seat in the benches there," he said with firm a stare, pointing at a booth with three rows of benches to his left. She didn't recognise the few that sat there, except for Constable Hamish. "Behind me is my solicitor, Mr Benjamin Cohan, but he prefers Benny. He'll be taking notes." His dark eyes peered at her as if she were a child about to venture into a pit of snakes. "This is a sensitive case. Don't say anything to anyone," he lifted his forefinger, "I mean it, Matilda. Whatever the prosecution says, you should say nothing, at all. He will offer his evidence and plead his case, then so shall I."

"Yes, I understand," said Matilda lowering her chin. She greeted Benny with a weak smile as she made her way to the booth. Listening to the murmuring in the room was suffocating and deafening. She stared at the boisterous people in the balconies dancing in high spirits and sharing callous laughter. Strangers were sharing the demise of an innocent man and she felt sick to her stomach.

Scraping and thudding reverberated across the room and the murmurs stopped. All arching their necks to catch sight of the murderer, who killed the diplomat. Matilda swallowed and sheer willpower stopped her from running over to him. Tears stung the back of her throat at the hollow sound of metal chains dragging along the floor. The chains rattled from the metal cuffs around Papa's wrists and ankles. The court martial with him pushed him forward with his black stick.

Her father was left standing and shackled inside the dock. There was no chair for him to sit. She scooted as close to the dock as she could, minimising eye contact with the barrister. There were three judges all dressed in the same black gowns and white wigs, except the wigs were larger and fancier with more rolled curls. They were seated on the main platform overlooking the court.

The middle judge had a fleshy face and ordered silence in a booming voice. He ordered the court usher to bring in the jury and within minutes shuffling and thumping of eighteen people entered a rectangular box and sat down.

The clerk rose from his seat and held a wad of papers in his hands. Lifting his chin and with a puffed chest, he read out the charges and Matilda's blood turned cold.

"The defendant, Mr Harold Wenslow, has been charged with the heinous crime of murder—"

The crowd blasted a dramatic gasp, followed by a wail. Matilda bit her lower lip.

"—of Mr Andrew Heslop, a diplomat in the service of Her Royal Highness, the Queen of England. What say you?" The clerk turned his hawk-like eyes towards her father.

Matilda's heart clenched at the forlorn look on her father's drawn, unshaven face. His matted hair covered the tips of his ears and she didn't recognise its colour.

"Not guilty!" Harold yelled with the confidence of a mighty army and the room burst into angry jeers. Elevating his chin, Harold gave Matilda a quick smile before glaring at the clerk, who glowered at him with disgust.

"Very well," the clerk said and turned to the judges with a quick nod before returning to his seat.

Matilda heard the judge with the fleshy face silence the crowd threatening to usher them out of the court and then he turned to the jury explaining their duties. Whenever her father gazed at her, Matilda mustered the bravest smile she could.

As the judge droned on, all she could think about was what would happen to her father, until at the mention of the prosecutor, Timothy Adams, her ears pricked.

She guessed the prosecutor couldn't be much older than her father and was dressed in the same attire as her barrister. His gown embraced him as he rose to his feet revealing a surprisingly podgy body. From Matilda's view, he appeared shorter than the average height of a man and wriggled his shoulders until his chest inflated.

"Your Honours and Jury of the court as the prosecuting solicitor, Timothy Adams, I shall prove beyond all doubt that the defendant is guilty of the crime of murder."

His first witness was Mr Benson, her father's manager and

Matilda winced, glancing at her father slouching in the dock. Couldn't the court give him a chair? Anyone could see he was exhausted.

"You are Peter Benson, are you not?" the prosecutor's voice said with a hint of condescension.

Peter nodded, "Yes, I am."

"Are you the owner of the construction company, Benson Builders?"

Peter responded the same.

"Can you tell me what happened on the fifth day of September in the year eighteen-eighty-two?"

Peter glanced at Harold with pity in his eyes and with reluctance proceeded to explain the day her father arrived at work drunk. She shrunk in her seat, tears welling up, knowing that Peter spoke the truth, but the prosecutor twisted his words as if her father had disrupted the business, which he had not. Peter tried to explain that was not the case, but the prosecutor didn't want to hear any more of it.

Matilda stared at George in horror. Why was he not saying anything? The little money she put together, she gave to him to represent her father. He remained silent watching the show as if enamoured like everybody else while his solicitor fervently scribbled at his desk.

The next two witnesses, she assumed had been at the tavern where the crime took place. Neither had seen her father push the diplomat that ended his life, but pointed at her father when the prosecutor asked them to identify the guilty person. There was no mention of the fourth person who argued with the diplomat.

"I rest my case. I have no more witnesses," the prosecutor said to the judges, and returned to his seat.

Flabbergasted, Matilda again stared at George, who this time jumped to his feet and relief washed over her.

"Your Honours," George said, introducing himself to the court. His self-assured voice rang through the courtroom. "The prosecution has not provided sufficient evidence to prove this innocent man is guilty and therefore has no case."

Matilda crossed her fingers and prayed. If the judges agreed, her father would be set free.

The judge steepled his fingers and glimpsed between the two gaudy-looking judges and they spoke in whispers.

The judge sat forward and said, "Your plea to the court is denied. Please go ahead and state your case to the jury."

George's shoulders slumped but gave a firm nod. He called Peter Benson as his witness, who described Harold Wenslow as a devoted employee and hard worker and the accident of her mother was explained to the court.

Matilda noticed the heart-wrenching look on her father's face and as much as she willed him to, he did not look in her direction.

Mam, Matilda thought as tears rolled down her eyes, *what would you think of all this?*

Satisfied, George thanked and excused Peter Benson only to call the previous two witnesses.

"Mr Garret Hudson," George said after confirming his name for the jury. "Were you present at the tavern on the night the diplomat was killed?"

Mr Hudson rolled his eyes and sighed, "Yes, you heard what I said already."

"How long were you there? At the tavern, I mean."

"Since the afternoon," Hudson admitted with pride. "I saw that man, the accused, he was there. He was drinking."

"Was anyone with you? Please repeat any answers that may seem you've answered with the prosecutor."

Mr Hudson huffed, "I told you already. The other witness is my friend."

"You were both drinking, weren't you?"

"Everyone drinks in a tavern or pub," Hudson guffawed. "Why else would anybody go there."

"So you admit you were both drunk or rather that you were not sober? I shall ask the same to your friend, the other witness."

"Uh-huh, well, I can't say," Hudson said, turning a shade of pink. "I don't remember. It's hazy."

"I see, so you were drunk, which would mean you cannot be certain that the accused had any dealings with the diplomat." George cleared his throat, and Matilda's heart soared when he added, "You didn't see a fourth patron, did you?"

Hudson paled and remained silent.

"I require you to answer the question, Mr Hudson." George paused for effect and said, "Remember, sir, you are under oath."

Hudson squirmed and gave a weak nod. "Yes, maybe... there might have been someone else."

"Might? You're not certain, but you think there was another man? The fourth man argued with the diplomat. You saw them argue, did you not?"

"I... uh," Hudson said, blabbering and appearing as if he were about to cry.

George smiled, thanked and excused Mr Hudson, calling the last witness.

Matilda exchanged a hopeful glance with her father, whose face had lit up. She peered at the prosecutor, who was running his fingers at the neckline of his gown.

"Mr Allan Solinski," George said in an amused tone. "The previous witness confirmed your presence at the same tavern and you were drinking with him, is that right?"

"I suppose, yeah," Solinski said with a drawl.

"Like your friend, Mr Hudson, you did see someone else

besides the accused at the tavern?" George said with a cocked brow. "May I remind you that you are under oath."

"Dunno, I mean, yeah there was someone and a fight... that man," Solinski pointed at Harold, "was sitting at the bar. Blimey all he had was a half glass of whiskey. T'was his second, I think."

"I see," George said, appearing uninterested. "Tell me, why would a diplomat venture into a tavern? Wouldn't you assume a diplomat would remain in the company of his companions?"

"Sometimes the rich folk like to see what happens in the lower towns," Solinski said, scratching the back of his ear, his face turned ashen. "What I meant to say is that maybe he had business..." he paused as he *um'd* and *ah'd*. "I made a mistake. I don't think he argued with anyone."

Surprise and elation filled George's face. "In that case, I may need to call in the owner of the tavern. You see I have a statement from him, which has been presented to the prosecutor and the court confirming who was in the tavern at the specified time."

Mr Solinski appeared defeated and his eyes lowered to his feet. "I dunno about anybody else. I have nothing more to say."

Matilda's heart soared as her barrister excused the witness. At first, she'd doubted George, but he was proving to be an excellent defence barrister. There was hope. The witnesses could not corroborate her father was guilty. She thought it was the opposite.

George's face crinkled with delight and he turned to the judges. "Your Honour, this is the end of the case of the defence. There is no evidence to prove that Harold Wenslow is guilty of the murder of Mr Andrew Henslop."

Excitement filled Matilda's heart and she didn't pay attention to the prosecutor or the defence barrister's closing speeches as they summed up their arguments. Surely they'd find her father innocent and investigate the identity of the fourth man.

The judge ordered the jury to leave the court and deliberate a decision in a specified room. Matilda snuck out of the booth and stood beside the dock.

"Papa, it looks good, doesn't it?" She said with an enormous grin, grabbing the wooden railing. "You'll be free."

Her father responded with a bold smile, but she noted the woeful expression on his face.

"What's wrong, Papa?"

"Matilda," he said in a hushed tone. The chains rattled and clanged as he tried to touch her face, but rested his hand over hers on the railing. "These proceedings are a ruse."

"Huh? What are you talking about?"

He sighed and his jaw tensed. Staring at her with tears in his eyes, he answered, "Someone high up is protecting someone. Whatever the outcome just know that I will always love you and I... I wish I had been strong for you... I better father..." his voice trailed off into soft sobs.

"No, Papa, George is a friend and you've seen how good he is."

"You better get back to your seat; it looks like the jury is coming back."

Her eyes widened. "Already? Does that mean it's good or bad?"

The chains rattled as he removed his hand and she noticed his raw skin beneath the shackles. Before she could utter another word, the judge ordered the court to settle down. Reluctantly, Matilda left her father's side and returned to her seat. Glancing at her father, her chest felt heavy as though her heart sunk towards the basement where the prisoners were gaoled.

"Jury foreperson, what say you in the matter of Harold

Wenslow standing trial by the prosecution for the murder of diplomat Andrew Henslop?"

Matilda's heart thumped watching one of the jury, a man dressed in a suit, rising to his feet. The room became stuffy and her gloves were hot. The man had a thick moustache, which moved as he spoke.

"Yes, Your Honour, we the jury have reached a decision," he said in a small voice. "We find the defendant —"

The world slowed down as Matilda stepped into a void she never knew existed and she shrieked at the man's last words.

"—guilty of murder."

The room exploded pouring cheers and applause as if an invisible curtain fell across the court room ending a winning theatre performance.

7
NEW BEGINNINGS

Matilda reached out for her father as the court officials hastily dragged her father from the dock, but he shook his head at her. Because of the crowd's reaction, the judges' decision to delay sentencing was unanimous.

She hurried to George and with tears rolling down her cheeks, she said, "Why did this happen? There is no proof... my father's innocent, you know that." He stared at her dismally as she clutched his arm. "Call a mistrial, you can do that, can't you?"

George pulled his arm away and sighed. "No, the best we can do is appeal. It will take months and maybe delay sentencing, but that is the only way."

"Is this justice?" Matilda said, her voice rising. "Sending an innocent man to gaol?"

George placed his hands over her shoulders and said, "I'm sorry. I'll inform you when I can set a date for another hearing, that is if the appeal is granted. They'll most likely send him to the Newgate Prison."

Disbelief overwhelmed her and she backed away, shaking

her head, ignoring George's multiple offers of sympathetic condolences. The room grew tight and suffocating. Matilda raced out of the courtroom, sobbing. How could this happen? First, she lost Mam and now Papa. It was not fair. How cruel could all these people be? Taking such joy and mirth over the misfortune of an innocent man's life; her father.

Pushing past the lingering crowd, she broke through the exit and breathed in the cool air, releasing her lungs from the putrid air of the courtroom. What was she going to do? She stood near a lamppost, out of the way of the spectators and as much as she tried, she couldn't stop crying. They hadn't given her the chance to say goodbye to Papa.

"May I ask what has distressed you?" a concerned, posh male voice said from beside her.

She glanced in the direction of the musical voice and a silken handkerchief with lace trimming dangled before her eyes.

"Please," the voice continued with kindness. "Take this. I don't mind."

"Thank you," Matilda said whimpering and accepting the handkerchief. She rubbed her fingers against the soft, smooth material before dabbing her eyes. She hadn't touched anything so delicate since her mother passed away.

He wore a black suit, a white double-breasted shirt and a black tie. She admired the shine of his raven hair combed into a side-parting and his sparkling eyes like dewdrops on bright green leaves after a rainy day. For a moment his friendly smile made her forget the heartbreak that besieged her.

"How rude of me," he said with the same smile, staring at her. "My name is Benedict Fawlson, It's all right if you don't feel comfortable telling me what's bothering you. I was hoping to help in some way if I could."

"Not at all," Matilda said, returning a weak smile and for the first time she felt hope.

"Matilda Wenslow," she said and noticed the interest on his masculine face. "My father has been wrongly accused of murder and he has been taken to prison. I don't know what to do. My barrister is a friend and thinks in a few months we can make a request for an appeal." She paused, drawing in a deep breath. "I'm alone now."

"I don't know how you can help me with that," she said, feeling relief at sharing the burden with someone, even if it was with a stranger.

Benedict was quiet and to her surprise, he'd paled. From his relaxed stance, he was now stiff and his arms crossed over his body with his hands gripping his arms. Had he attended the court trial and thought her father was guilty despite the conflicting evidence?

His jaw tensed as he pressed his lips. With a furtive glance at her, he said, "You're right. I'm truly sorry for all you've gone through. This is something I cannot help you with. If you'll excuse me, I have a prior arrangement I just remembered. I should make it on time if I leave now. He tipped his black hat. "Have a good day, Miss Wenslow."

Matilda stared after him, agape. Realising she still had his silk handkerchief, which had his initials embroidered in gold, she tried to call out to him, but he'd disappeared. What just happened? That fleeting moment of hope vanished and sadness pumped into her heart.

Closing her eyes, she steadied her heaving chest by drawing in slow breaths and exhaling. All she could do was return to the bleak, empty house in Whitechapel.

MATILDA STARED at the letter in her lap and didn't know what to make of it. Moments ago, Peter Benson had left, giving her time to reflect on his offer. He'd jotted it all down in a letter as if to make his proposal official. Did Papa know about Mr Benson's suggestion?

She placed the letter aside on a small table, walked to the cast iron stove and lit it, placing a pot of water on top. Rubbing her arms she disappeared into the kitchen and dug in the cupboard for a teacup.

Papa's absence hurt. Every time there was a knock at the door or a rattle of the doorknob, her heart lifted with anticipation thinking her father had come home. Ever since he'd been whisked off to prison, the house seemed darker.

As Matilda brewed tea, she recalled Mr Benson's visit and shivers ran down her spine. He'd been dressed in brown trousers and a white button-up shirt, a coat folded over his arm and she assumed he came to her before going to work.

"Your father and I go way back and have been close, you know," Peter had said. He didn't take off his hat when he entered the house and it disgusted her when he seated himself without her invitation.

"Thank you for trying to help him," Matilda said, closing the door behind him. All she had wanted was to bask in solitude. Entertaining visitors was not on her list.

He upturned his hands, palms facing the ceiling. "I do what I can." He lifted his arm, elbow resting over the top of the chair.

Although he owned the house, Matilda decided his sudden appearance and familiarity was in poor taste. It was her home. How could he waltz in and act as if he owned everything?

"How can I help you, Mr Benson?" Matilda said, taking a seat opposite him.

"Oh, Peter, if you will."

"Thank you, but given the circumstances, I feel that it is

improper to address my father's employer as such, Mr Benson," Matilda said, ignoring the rush of adrenaline through her body. What was he doing here?

"I had a word with your father some time ago," he said as if reading her mind, and eyed the chairs, the frames on the walls and the peeling paint. "He somewhat agreed to terms for re-employment, but I doubt he remembers."

Peter stared at her with a toothy grin. She swallowed and gripped the edges of the seat, glancing at the door.

"And what was the agreement?"

He dug into his coat pocket and pulled out the letter, which she hesitantly accepted from him.

"You're a pretty lass. You shouldn't be living here," he said in a casual tone that Matilda thought was inappropriate.

"Mr Benson, I am happy to stay here even without my father. Unless you want me to leave and go elsewhere?" Matilda's heart had pulsated and her skin grew clammy. It may not be the best place to live, but she had nowhere else to go.

"I'd like to make you my wife," he blurted, leaning forward, his arms hung over his legs. "Who knows how long your father is gonna stay in prison? I've been a bachelor long enough. I think I'm ready to move on, you know. My wife died five or six years ago."

Matilda felt her blood turn cold. Would Papa do that to her? No, he wouldn't marry her off; especially not to someone who was a few years older than he himself.

Her mind raced and said, "Thank you, Mr Benson, but I don't think it's a good idea. The last thing on my mind is marriage. I'm sure you can understand that it's only been a day since my father's trial. He hasn't been sentenced yet."

"Fair enough," he said, jerking his head towards the letter. "Everything's in there. It's official when you're ready, all right?"

Speechless, Matilda's stomach turned and she drew in a quick breath. At first, she hadn't taken him seriously, but he appeared convinced. She lifted her chin and feigned a smile.

"I'll need to have a word with my father when I am permitted to visit him," Matilda said, unable to hold back her disdain. Did he expect her to repay his kindness through marriage? The idea was absurd.

He didn't leave quick enough for her, but when he did she locked the door.

There was one part out of everything that Mr Benson was correct and that was she couldn't stay at this house any longer. With her father in prison and no money coming in it was not possible for her to survive. Marriage was out of the question, especially not to him.

Sitting on the couch, she sipped her piping hot tea and blew at the wisps of steam. She closed her eyes and reopened them hoping she'd find everything since the passing of her mother had been a vicious nightmare. But it wasn't, it was real. This was her life now.

If she remained at the house, Mr Benson would certainly come around again. She remembered while growing up that one of her friends had to find work to support themselves after suffering the loss of their only relative.

A smile tugged at her lips, she would do the same. There were many people in the area she'd come to know and she still had friends from her old life. Perhaps if she asked around and made house calls, she would find work at an inn, a helper at a store or work as a maid. She refused to live in pity anymore.

Matilda gulped her cup of tea and rose to her feet. After rinsing her teacup in the kitchen, she grabbed her coat and headed out the door.

8
THE MANOR

Matilda's eyes widened at the sight of Burlington Manor in Mayfair. The magnificent white three-story home boasted its Victorian charm with its steep gabled roofs and high round towers peaking the blue sky. Matilda admired the bay windows on the first floor, which she knew was the parlour.

The beautiful garden was decorated in bright colours among a mass of green. It was enclosed by a black steel fence and she pushed open the charming gate, cold to the touch, allowing it to close behind her. As she walked towards the entrance she breathed in the fresh scents of various flowers.

Her heart beat faster as she approached the stairs, which had a glistening balustrade rail and opened into an enormous verandah. Taking a deep breath, she knocked on the door and waited. The minutes seemed like hours, but she knew Miss Amelia Thames was expecting her.

The door creaked open and the butler, Mr Penn, glanced down and greeted her with a cheerful smile. As she expected his pencil-shaped moustache did not move. She knew it was a silly thought, but it must be glued on. He was dressed in a fancy black suit, pressed white shirt and bow tie.

"Ah, good show, Miss Wenslow," he said in a baritone voice. "Miss Thames will be pleased. She doesn't like tardiness and you are early. Mr and Mrs Burlington are out and will not see you."

"Thank you, Mr Penn," Matilda said, returning a beaming smile. She walked inside the hallway and admired the dark wood ornately decorated. She couldn't imagine why the ceilings had to be so high because she'd never met anyone quite so tall. Opposite the closed parlour door, to her right, a gold-framed painting had been hung and she blushed. It was of a woman and a man in a conservatory revealing too much skin for her taste.

Soft footfalls caught Matilda's attention and she examined Miss Thames approaching her from the lavish carpeted staircase. She was immaculate in her housekeeper's uniform; a long-sleeved, high-collared pristine black dress covered by a white apron with lace trimming.

Miss Thames clapped her hands with delight, but she didn't smile. "Good, you did well coming early on your first day." She turned to Mr. Penn and thanked him before beckoning Matilda to follow her.

"Matilda, you'll be wearing a white and red striped dress and remain in the scullery. You'll answer to Mrs McElfroy, the cook, but you'll report everything through Miss Abby Tate, the kitchen maid. Understood?"

"Yes," Matilda answered with a nod. Miss Thames was gifted with speech and made her points clear at the speed of a locomotive. Matilda's uniform and apron would be on her cot, a shared space with the other maids on the third floor.

"...you'll address Mr. Penn and me as you do already, the other servants by their Christian names, except for the cook.

Mr and Mrs Burlington will be Sir and Ma'am, though I doubt you'll see much of them. Their daughter, Miss Joan is well-behaved, but a sixteen-year-old girl, well..." she paused and gazed at Matilda, holding a medium-sized weather-beaten brown suitcase. "Is that all you have?"

Matilda nodded. Before she gave notice of vacating the house to Mr Benson, she had sold everything. It broke her heart to sell what was left of her old life, but she had no choice. Her father would have agreed.

"You have nothing of value?"

"I have some jewellery that belonged to my mother," Matilda said, her voice shaky at the memory of her mother wearing them.

"All right, good. Best to declare them," said Miss Thames with a raised brow. "Everything in this house is of high value and you don't want to be caught having valuables." She held out her hand. "Hand them over to me, I'll keep them safe."

Matilda turned ashen and felt as though the roof collapsed on her. "What? Why? Can't I keep them in my suitcase?"

Miss Thames sighed, "Matilda, your possessions are safer with me, I promise. You can have them at any time, but you won't be wearing them while on duty now, will you?"

Matilda's heart thumped and she choked down tears, but she knew Miss Thames was right. She unclipped her suitcase and dug inside pulling out her mother's jewellery and with reluctance handed them over.

"Absolutely beautiful," Miss Thames said with a reassuring smile. "Your mother had exquisite taste, didn't she?"

Matilda couldn't find the words to answer and nodded with a weak smile. Watching Miss Thames place the jewellery inside her dress pocket felt like someone had dug into her chest, ripping out her heart.

"Let's continue shall we?" Miss Thames said. It was not a

question. Matilda held onto her bag and followed her through the secret hallways that maids needed to use to stay out of sight and complete their daily routines.

The kitchen was enormous. Panelled cupboards with shelves lined the walls surrounding a massive highly polished kitchen table. The pots and pans gleamed. Miss Thames introduced Matilda to the cook and the kitchen maid, who welcomed her with warm smiles.

"The scullery is through that door," Miss Thames pointed to an open door located near the back door. "It must be clean at all times, and all metallic and earthenware must be scrubbed. When Mrs McElfroy and Abbey are having their meals you need to keep watch so the food doesn't burn. Abbey will advise you on the rest of the chores. You'll do as she says."

"I understand and thank you," Matilda replied. She was drained listening to Miss Thames and walking around the house even if it was only the secret hallways. She didn't realise just how vast the house was.

"Good," Miss Thames said, offering a pleasant smile. "Allow me to be the first to welcome you to Burlington Manor. But, first, let's get you into uniform."

Matilda summoned another smile and followed Miss Thames to the third floor, the upper and topmost floor where she would spend her nights in exhaustion.

~

TWO WEEKS HAD PASSED and Matilda's body throbbed every day after working in the scullery. She cleaned and scoured the floor, work surfaces, stove, sink, endless pots and pans, cutlery and plates. She'd clear away the leftovers, ensuring garbage was thrown out.

Every morning, before Mrs McElfroy came down to the

kitchen, she ensured the stove was lit, and that there was sufficient hot water for tea and washing. The maintenance man, Mr Williams, came early to drop off coal, and firewood and repair anything that broke. He was a man of few words and Matilda didn't press him for conversation.

The days were endless tasks, but she enjoyed working with Abbey and Mrs McElfroy and appreciated her work, despite how strenuous it became. Miss Thames would check on her and engage in a playful conversation when it was only them. Matilda felt comfortable with Miss Thames and trusted her as she would a sister.

When she woke up and stretched out her stiff arms, she thought over the day to come and smiled. After she completed her tasks after breakfast, she would go visit her father at Newgate Prison. She didn't tell anyone other than Miss Thames, Abbey and Mrs McElfroy about him. They knew if word got out, it wouldn't be good for the Burlington's reputation and what it would mean for her. Matilda was confident her secret was safe.

As she scrubbed and performed her tasks, excitement welled from her belly as every duty completed meant time was ticking for her to see her father. She hadn't seen him in weeks and she was eager to tell him everything since they'd been separated.

Once she'd placed the last plate on the rack, Abbey gave her permission to leave. Matilda dried her hands and her heart raced as she hurried to the third floor to wash up and change into her best clothing. She bought a purple dress a week ago with ruffled sleeves, the kind her mother had loved.

She left the house through the servants' entrance at the back of the house and caught a stagecoach to take her to the prison. Staring out the window, Matilda was reminded of the life she'd escaped and gazed at the children playing in the streets, people wearing old, worn-out clothes as they performed their tasks or couldn't afford to buy clothes.

The stagecoach came to a stop outside Newgate Prison. Walking towards the entrance, she noticed the gallows where criminals were hanged for the public eye, but this ended about fifty years ago. At the thought of her father being hanged, Matilda shivered.

The door was ominous and gave the same steely impression of the prison, its stone bricks were dull and intimidating. She lifted the heavy black knocker and it smashed against the steel with the sound of a cannon. She drew in a deep breath as if preventing the door from sucking her into an abyss. It groaned as it opened and a tall man dressed in a black uniform with buttons on his tunic and a black hat.

"Yes?" the man's voice boomed with annoyance.

"I'm here to see my father, Harold Wenslow," said Matilda and swallowed. Beads of cold sweat slipped down her temple and she swiped it with shaky hands. She'd heard terrible stories about the prison and had no idea what to expect. Only the worst type of criminals came to Newgate Prison.

Was she risking her life to visit her father? She determined it didn't matter as long as she saw him again.

"Inside," the man ordered without introducing himself. "Sign the book."

Matilda clasped her hands and entered, grimacing at the bang behind her. The room was dark and glum with nothing other than the moist stones that enclosed her and a rectangular table with a chair. She walked to the table and found a dog-eared book its pages were yellowed. After scribbling her name, she returned to the man.

He beckoned her to follow him and led her down a narrow corridor. She noticed small booths on either side of the bar covered by a grate. Another guard was leaning against the stone wall at the end of the corridor as if waiting for her. The void in the corridor was filled by the murmuring of the other visitors. Squeezing past them the guard at the end gave a quick nod and he appeared less friendly than the first man.

"Wait there," the guard said in a firm tone, pointing at a tiny space between a giant of a man and an old woman.

Thanking him, Matilda squeezed past them and waited in her booth; it seemed like hours.

A dragging thud followed by the shrieking of shackles and chains grinding against the stone floor seized the chattering. It was her father and tears pricked her eyes. How could he be chained up?

His eyes turned moist when he saw her and warmth filled her heart. Tears of joy rolled down her cheeks.

"Papa, I..." she choked over her words, gripping the grated bars. "Why are you chained like that?"

He appeared defeated and shook his head with a heavy shrug.

"I have so much to tell you and I miss you." Although she knew he didn't want her to pity him, she did. He didn't deserve this kind of treatment nor did he belong in this dreadful place.

At every step, he huffed and she noticed his scrawny appearance. Murmurs and chattering started again when the sound of her father's chains seized when he sat at the booth on his side.

"How are you?" Harold said with a wan smile, but his eyes glistened.

Matilda wiped her eyes and told him everything from the end of the trial to Mr Benson's inappropriate proposal.

Harold shook his head in disgust, "I can't believe he did that to you. Tell me about your employer, are they good to you?"

Matilda bobbed her head, "Yes, the house is amazing. The

work is tough, as a scullery maid, but I work with wonderful people. The house belongs Mr Oscar Burlington, he's a successful financial businessman and his wife's name is Margaret. I haven't met them. Servants aren't supposed to talk to the family. They have a daughter, Miss Joan."

"I'm proud of you," Harold grinned, trying to push his fingers between the tightly spaced bars. "Your mother would have been, too. You've done well."

"What is it like here?" Matilda glanced at the guard, who was observing everyone as a predator would pounce on its prey. "I have heard terrible stories."

"Yes, it's been tough here. People accused of murder are treated..." his voice was croaky and he trailed off. "It's not the same as others. We don't get as much free time in the yard. I share a cell with others, some are sick. I stay away from them."

"You're not sick, are you?" Matilda's eyes widened and her heart thumped. Doctors seldom visited prisons.

Harold flashed another grin, forming lines around his eyes and he lifted his arm. "Your papa is strong. I won't get sick that easy. We work long hours here. George came to see me and he managed to postpone sentencing again. The diplomat's family...well, they want me in the gallows."

Matilda's hand flew to her mouth. "No! That can't happen, you're innocent."

Sharp clanging and tinging resonated from the bars and Matilda covered her ears.

"Time's up!" the guard shouted. "Get going."

"No, the time is not enough," said Matilda making eye contact with her father and her heart felt crushed observing the pain in his eyes.

"Come again, honey," Harold said with a frown and his lips pressed together. "I'll not be going anywhere soon," he added with a smile, but she noticed the distress behind his smile. He didn't want her to leave either.

"I will, Papa," Matilda said.

"I love you," he said.

"I love you, too." She watched a guard grab her father by his shoulders and tears streamed down her cheeks. "Bye, I'll see you again. I miss you," she said, her voice rising at the sound of the chains and shackles.

"Miss, get going," the guard ordered.

Matilda grasped her skirt, tears spilling over onto her dress. With a heavy heart, she obeyed and followed everyone, leaving her father behind and alone.

9
UNEXPECTED VISITOR

NINE MONTHS LATER

It was still dark when Matilda woke up and she jumped out of bed. She loved listening to the crickets trilling accompanied by the caw-caw of the birds. After braiding her hair, she wrapped a white headscarf over her head. She pulled her pinafore over her black long-sleeved dress tying a knot at the back. She reflected on her accomplishments in the house and now held the position of a housemaid. Mrs McElfroy and Abby had become close friends and spoke highly of Matilda. This pleased Miss Thames, who watched her and promoted her.

Abby was happy to continue working in the kitchen and appeared to be happier than Matilda at the news of her promotion. During meals and in between work, Matilda was thrilled to spend time with the rest of the staff as equals and she now shared a finer room with three other maids. A new girl, Emily, had taken over the role of the scullery maid and Matilda taught her everything she knew.

She hurried to the parlour, opened the shutters and began

to clean the room, while the other maids began their duties in other rooms. Once Mr and Mrs Burlington and Miss Joan woke and were ready for breakfast, she'd go upstairs and start to clean Miss Joan's room. Some days Miss Joan wanted to lie in bed longer and Matilda would have to return later; she hoped this was not the case. Miss Joan was prone to her morning moodiness, but it didn't take long for Matilda to understand that a glass of orange juice brightened the girl's mood.

"Good Morning, Miss Joan," said Matilda with a polite smile, admiring her white ruffled dress narrowed in a V-shape at the waist trimmed with gold lace. "You look beautiful today."

Miss Joan stared at her quizzically as she always did, but thanked her. She lifted her chin and with a poised stance, she walked past Matilda in the hallway and descended the stairs. She entered Miss Joan's massive room and greeted Lydia, the Lady's Maid, who was at the dressing table cleaning up pins, combs and other paraphernalia.

In the centre of the room was a double-sized four-poster bed with drapes. Matilda placed the new linen she held on a chair and began to make the bed.

"It's your birthday, isn't it?" Lydia said looking up at Matilda while she neatened the table.

"Yes," Matilda said with a bright smile, surprised that Lydia remembered. Although they crossed paths, Lydia was not one for conversations. "Miss Thames has allowed me to take the afternoon off."

"That's wonderful, I hope you enjoy your birthday. You're going to spend the afternoon with someone special?"

Joy poured into Matilda's heart and she answered, "Yes. I can't imagine spending my birthday with anyone else."

Lydia responded with a sweet smile and resumed her task leaving Matilda to clean the room, the fireplace grate, sweeping the ash and the luxurious carpet. Matilda couldn't help smiling. What a better way than to spend her eighteenth birthday with her father even though it would be at Newgate Prison?

~

Matilda knew the rules of the prison and was thankful that the diplomat's family had forgotten about her father; according to George. They stopped pressing for the gallows and were satisfied for him to be left to rot at Newgate.

Mrs McElfroy had baked a loaf of Parkin, a gingerbread cake made with oatmeal and black treacle, that she could share with her father. The guards usually didn't allow visitors to bring in food and treats, but seeing as she visited her father monthly and Matilda cut up a few slices for them, they happily obliged.

"This tastes good," Harold said taking a bite. He closed his eyes and Matilda watched his face light up with pure delight. Mrs McElfroy was a genius and Matilda told her so, regularly. It had the perfect blend of ginger and sweet treacle.

"Happy birthday, honey," her father said, gesturing for another slice. "I'm honoured you chose to spend it with me."

"I can't imagine being anywhere else," said Matilda with a giggle, exhilarated to see him enjoy the treat she brought. She didn't think the guards would've allowed it, but she was relieved they permitted this small luxury. He was no longer chained and shackled.

"You're still happy working for the Burlingtons?"

"Yes, the job is demanding at times and Miss Joan can be difficult, but she's kind, too. Many of the staff aren't fond of her, but I think she's misunderstood."

Harold smiled and lines appeared over his forehead and at

the corners of his eyes. "You have a good heart, Matilda. You see the best in people even when they don't deserve it. I wish I could've been a better father. I know better now... I just wish I could make it up to you, somehow."

"It's all right, Papa," Matilda insisted. "Let's talk about good things. We've survived this far. Whatever comes our way, we can endure it together, can't we?"

"Yes, of course. You're right," he said, leaning forward he added, "I've been thinking. I don't want you to hold your life back because of me."

Matilda stared at him with a surprised frown.

"I don't want you wasting your time and money visiting me every month and forgetting to have a life of your own. I want you to meet someone special and marry... have children and watch them grow up. I've lived and I want you to live a happy life."

"Papa..." Matilda couldn't finish her sentence. Didn't he want her to visit him anymore? "I won't abandon you—"

"No, that's not what I'm saying," he said with a sigh. "Please, if a suitable man takes to your liking, you have my blessing, that's all."

Blushing, Matilda nodded. She didn't know what to say other than, "Yes, Papa."

She always thought the visits were too short, but on this day, the guards gave them extra time for which she was grateful. As she left, the guards wished her a happy birthday.

∼

FATIGUE CRAWLED over her shoulders as she returned to Burlington Manor. She found it tiring whenever she travelled to London City. It was quiet and serene in Mayfair, not like the lively and bustling streets of London.

Matilda entered through the servants' entryway and made her way towards her room, she noticed a familiar man sitting in the parlour enjoying a cup of tea. As if in a trance she entered the room and he raised his head, staring at her in astonishment.

"Benedict, is it really you?"

He swiftly stood to his feet and bowed. "I didn't know you were a resident of the Burlingtons, please excuse my poor manners, Miss Matilda."

Matilda smiled and her stomach flip-flopped knowing he remembered her.

"No," she responded and turned bashful. "I... I've been working here as a maid. I'm off duty though. How is it that you're here?"

She swallowed and lifted her chin mesmerised once again by his dazzling eyes. Through the bay windows, the sunlight shone over him like a crown above his head. She exhaled a silent sigh to steady her thumping heart. Why was she behaving this way around him? It was embarrassing and she prayed he didn't notice.

He rubbed his hand over his stubbled chin and glanced around the room.

"My father, Mr Bertrand Fawlson," he paused, "have you heard of him?"

"No, I haven't," Matilda said with a shake of her head, wishing that she had.

"Oh, well, he has business with Mr Burlington and desires me to learn the business to take it over when he retires. I'm not one for socialising and such, but he is convinced it is important and that I should familiarise myself with it in order to engage in negotiations. Another area I'm not particularly fond of."

"I see. I think I understand," Matilda answered, remembering how her mother would spend hours on end engaging and hosting events for the community and the chapel. "I've had some experience with socialising. It's tiring, isn't it?"

Benedict stared at her with relief and he exhaled a sharp breath. "Thank you, at least there's someone who knows what I'm talking about." He offered a charming light chuckle.

Matilda couldn't look away from him and he didn't avoid eye contact either. Silence filled the room and she felt a strange, but warm sensation fall upon her. There was something about him that captivated and fascinated her.

His jaw tensed and he swallowed. As he was about to say something it was lost at the familiar sound of Miss Thames's footsteps entering the parlour. Instantly, the sensation disappeared, but her heart raced.

"Oh, Matilda," Miss Thames said in surprise. "I didn't expect to see you." She glanced from Matilda to Benedict, whose cheeks had reddened. Matilda thought it was from the sun. "Do you know each other?"

"Yes, but we met a while back. It was a brief encounter," Matilda chimed with a calming smile.

The corners of Miss Thames's mouth tipped upward.

Hearty laughter and thudding footsteps stopped at the parlour entrance and the laughter ended. The air became cold and awkward. Miss Thames appeared uncomfortable.

Matilda was familiar with Mr Burlington and for the first time, she shrunk under the gaze of his dark eyes. Both men were dressed in black suits with ties.

Mr Burlington shot Miss Thames a confused and dark look. Matilda knew she shouldn't be there, but now that she was, what would he do?

Benedict cleared his throat, which broke the awkward silence. "Father, may I introduce you to Miss Matilda Wenslow," he raised a brow gesturing his hand towards her.

"Miss Matilda, I'm honoured to introduce my father, Mr Fawlson."

"Delighted to meet you," Matilda responded with a warm smile. She avoided Mr Burlington's stare and guilt overcame her at the thought of him reprimanding Miss Thames once they left. Even though she was not dressed in her maid's attire, she was certain Benedict's father knew she was not a resident of the house. After all, her dress was not in style and she could not compare to Miss Joan.

Mr Fawlson glowered at her through similar, but unappealing green eyes. He eyed her with disdain and glimpsed at his son with disapproval.

"Hmm, so this is what my son gets up to while I'm away," he scoffed and turned to Mr Burlington as if she were invisible. "I look forward to our next meeting." With a stiff smile, he offered his hand, which Mr Burlington accepted.

"In the future, my son shall be involved in all my business affairs. He is my heir and as you know will take over the business."

Without a glance in Matilda's direction, Mr Fawlson said, "Benedict our business is concluded here. We need to leave for our next appointment." He turned on his heels but sideglanced an angry stare at Matilda before he left the parlour, accompanied by Mr Burlington.

"Forgive my father, Matilda," Benedict said, his voice was smooth and full of compassion. "He was rude and I apologise on his behalf."

"It's all right, I understand," Matilda responded, smiling from her heart. "He is a businessman and I am a maid. Perhaps at one time, if we met sooner, he would've been courteous."

"It was good to see you again," he said and bowed, flashing his charming smile that creased his cheeks. The word that came to her mind was handsome.

"And, you. I never expected to see you again, but here you were," Matilda said with a soft chortle.

His eyes lingered on her and with a brief nod, like he'd done on that day they first met, he hastily disappeared to join his father.

Matilda's heart fluttered. She hadn't noticed Miss Thames was still in the room.

"Are you planning to stand there and gaze out the window for the entire day?" Miss Thames asked in a humorous tone.

Returning from her dream state, her cheeks grew hot, and glimpsed at Miss Thames, who gazed at her with a strange look in her eyes.

"No, I'm sorry. I was on my way to get dressed into my uniform and then I saw Benedict, uh, Mr Fawlson." Her heart beat faster and she couldn't apologise enough and hurried out of the parlour.

Matilda's steps were light as she climbed the stairs as if walking on clouds. The warm sensation she felt in the parlour returned as she thought of Benedict. How long had he been visiting the Burlington Manor while she scrubbed and scoured the scullery, and washed pots and pans? And now, of all times, as a housemaid, they crossed paths again.

Did he remember their conversation at the courthouse? He must, if he remembered her name. She remembered what her father told her at the prison and heat rose from her neck to her cheeks. Should she tell her father about Benedict?

She didn't know how long it took for her to redress into her uniform. The air was light, and she gazed at the clouds through her bedroom window, imagining she was floating above them. Stepping away from the window, she exhaled a gentle sigh. Did it all matter? Would she see him again? If so, nothing could ever happen between them. It was evident that his father didn't approve of her.

Nevertheless, a smile tugged at her lips and she wondered what her mother would say if she were alive. Matilda imagined her mother telling her anything was possible. She had heard the love story between her parents and how she gave up a life of prestige for love and happiness.

Matilda left her room and her mind was flooded with stories her parents shared with her as a young girl and she'd come to believe that love was magical. Did she find that same magic with Benedict? Did he feel it, too, or was it all just in her mind?

Skipping down the stairs, Matilda's heart soared, and decided she didn't care. It was a wonderful dream that she would keep in her heart forever.

10
FLOURISHING HEARTS

Matilda groaned as she stretched her back leaning as far back as possible with outstretched arms. Changing bed sheets, sweeping the floor, tending to the fireplace, and cleaning the master bedroom were an arduous task for its massive size. She walked downstairs, holding dirty sheets in her arms, she was stunned to see Benedict wandering around the house. She didn't expect to see him again.

"Mr. Fawlson, what brings you here? I didn't think I'd see you so soon," she said, and her cheeks flushed.

"Ah, Miss Matilda, please call me, Benedict," he said.

"Do you think that is proper?" she stated and glanced around the hallway. "Miss Thames or my Master would be horrified to hear me address you casually."

"You're right, of course. How insensible of me," he said appearing uncomfortable in his clothes. Pulling on his sleeves, adjusting his high-collared double-breasted shirt and bowtie. He offered an apologetic smile. "Would you mind indulging when no one is around?"

"Mr. Fawlson, I can't do that." Her heart beat faster at his intense gaze, and she lowered her chin. "I need to get the linen to the laundry because they are waiting for me."

He moved aside and stared at the painting in the hallway. "What do you think the artist was thinking when painting that picture."

Matilda couldn't look at that picture and kept staring at her feet. "I don't know. How could I? I was not with the artist when it was painted."

Benedict glanced at her with amusement and he chortled. "I was wondering what you thought about it."

"How could a simple maid provide such an answer?"

"Miss Matilda, we both know you're not a simple maid, am I wrong?"

"Mr. Fawlson, the picture does not suit my taste in art. I fear it reveals too much skin… and, it lacks proper clothing. Why anyone should paint or admire such a piece is beyond my understanding."

"You don't approve?"

Matilda shook her head, "Without a doubt, no. It is improper, but not my place to offer my opinion to the Master or his wife. Not even Miss Joan is fazed by it," she paused, "please, Mr. Fawlson, I need to perform my duties on time."

"That's fine," he gave a curt nod. "I shall be waiting in the drawing room. There should be tea and biscuits."

Her head whipped up and she swallowed at his lop-sided grin. With or without his hat, he was dashing, and compared to his father, he was even-tempered and didn't care for airs and graces. Surely, he hadn't come here to see her.

"Are you here to see, Miss Joan?" Matilda said as she stepped further down the hallway, and hurried to get as far away from him as she could.

Nothing had been declared to the Master and she had no intention of causing trouble to the Burlingtons. They'd been kind to her and such dealings with Mr. Fawlson would create slanderous gossip.

"Miss Joan?" his smile broadened. "I believe she is with her governess and I don't intend on calling on a sixteen-year-old girl. It's business. You'll see more of me and my father. The business is flourishing as we enter international agreements. I abhor standing in one place for extended periods."

"I see," Matilda acknowledged with a polite smile. "Then I suppose when the time comes when I clean the drawing room, I will find you there?"

His shoulder twitched into a shrug and his brows raised, "Perhaps, you might. I can't say. However..." his voice trailed off, and she held her breath as he stared into her eyes, she was paralysed. She never noticed his long eyelashes.

"...we could bump into each another as one might say."

"You're teasing me," Matilda inhaled, unable to break eye contact. "I have work to do. Good day, Mr. Fawlson."

"Good day," she heard him say in a gentle voice. She didn't look back, but his steps echoed toward the drawing room, and she gasped for air not realising she'd been holding her breath.

"Was that Mr. Benedit Fawlson?" she heard Miss Thames' voice. It was as though she could feel her breath against her neck.

Matilda spun around, her heart racing in her head. "I suppose it was, I think so," her face reddened. "I heard him say he and his father were here on business."

"I heard the same, but that was yesterday," she grinned with a curious look in her eyes. "There was much said and does that painting make you uncomfortable?"

"Please, Miss Thames, I need to get these sheets to laundry," Matilda said, touching her throat and avoiding eye contact.

"I don't need to declare anything to the Master of the

house. You're under my observation and my responsibility. As long as you adhere to code, I won't stand in your way."

"In my way? I don't understand?"

"Take those sheets to laundry, before Miss Canning loses her noodles," Miss Thames said with a quiet, intrigued chuckle as she sauntered away.

Matilda's brows furrowed. Did Miss Thames hear the entire conversation? Matilda's instinct gave her the impression that Miss Thames knew something she failed to understand. Heading down the narrow stairs to the laundry, her body was shaking. It was the same when she first met him, and every other time. Why did he have this affect on her? Was there something wrong with her? She had never experienced this reaction with any other man before.

Rushing into the laundry room, she handed over the sheets, noticing Miss Canning's red puffed-up face, and swiftly departed. She hadn't delivered the sheets late. It wasn't her fault that Benedi-Mr Fawlson appeared from nowhere saying he was on business."

She didn't know what to think. Didn't it make sense for Mr Fawlson to call on Miss Joan? Though young, she was striking and overheard Mr Burlington in his study denying a betrothal with his daughter.

Despite the apprehensive that swirled in her stomach, a desire to clean the drawing room at that moment was tempting; however, it was not her day to clean the room. She shook her head, it was a silly notion. An aristocrat's son courting a maid was unthinkable. It did not happen so easily.

∽

Matilda attempted to hide from Benedict and Mr Fawlson as much as possible. She swapped duties, but Miss Thames scolded her every time she found out. She was relieved to have been tasked to clean the study after the Fawlson's met with Mr Burlington as they would all have left.

Stretching on her tip-toes, she lifted her right arm and dusted the top of the bookshelf with a feather duster. Unable to reach the top, she pulled up a chair and stood on it. She blew out an air of frustration. The chair didn't help much. As she tapped the top of the shelf, her balance shifted and panic set in her arms flapping in the air. Drawing in an emergency breath of air in preparation for a painful collision with the extravagant green carpet. Closing her eyes, the world paused, and confusion filled her mind as her body drifted in the air.

Turning her head, her eyes grew like saucers as she stared into Benedict's pinched face, full of worry. His arms were tight around her waist and she feared if she exhaled, the moment would be lost. Blood rushed in her ears, her eyes palpitated, and his eyes had never appeared greener.

"Are you all right?" he said, and she nodded.

Helping her to regain balance he said, "That was awfully dangerous. What made you think to climb a chair?"

She rubbed the back of her head, and gave a sheepish smile, averting his gaze. "I couldn't reach the top and the other maids stood on chairs. I didn't know the top shelf was so high."

"You could have hurt yourself," he said, lowering his head as if inspecting her face for injuries. "I was worried." He stood to his full height and she lifted her chin, gazing at him.

"I'm fine, thank you," she said, placing her hand over her racing heart. She hadn't heard him enter the study. "A bit out of breath for shock, but I'm fine. Thank you, Bene—Mr Fawlson."

A cheeky lop-sided grin appeared on his face, but he said nothing.

"What are you doing here? Hasn't your meeting with Mr Burlington ended?"

"Yes, it has. But I don't care for loitering around the gentleman's club. The smell sickens me." He stared at her with the same smile. "Why would I seek company with a group of men discussing issues that don't concern me when I can find a better company here?"

Matilda flushed. Was he talking about her? She recalled his answer when she inquired whether he'd come to see Miss Joan.

"Does Miss Thames know you're here?"

"Yes, of course. It would be rude to not inform her, wouldn't it?" He held out his arm, and said, "Miss Thames told me where to find you. Please do me the honour and walk with me to the back garden. I believe you know of a secret entrance."

Matilda gaped at him. Miss Thames told him where to find her. Was she aware Benedict was following her around? Though, whenever she saw him her heart skipped a beat. He was breathtaking.

Shaking her head, she responded in amazement, "Did Miss Thames tell you about the back garden? It's only for servants. If Mr Burlington or your father were to find out—"

"They will not," his voice was confident and he nudged his arm against hers. "Well? Will you take a walk with me? I hear it's stunning at this time of day."

Uncertain, she enveloped her arm around his. He led her out of the study and she lowered her face to her feet, shielding her face with her hand. What if someone were to see her? Miss Joan would never keep quiet.

"I don't think—"

"We're here," he announced as they walked through the entrance that led towards the servants' quarter, past the kitchen and down the unsteady stairs to the garden.

Benedict was right. She'd been to the garden many times,

how was it that on this occasion the table beneath the gazebo was laden with snacks and lemonade?

"It's tea time, I believe," Benedict said with a proud smirk. "I hope you're surprised," he chuckled, "you are surprised. I'm pleased."

"Join me for tea?"

Deciding she had no choice in the matter, Matilda's heart soared as she nodded.

∼

Matilda hadn't seen Benedict since having tea with him, which had been a week ago. Disappointment and concern swept through her mind. Without reason, he'd stay behind after business meetings or he'd come during the week and surprise her.

She sat with the other maids in the servants' dining hall, drinking tea and enjoying a side of roasted lamb. She missed his annoying, charming company, and smiled.

"What's on your mind?" Miss Thames inquired, and Matilda rushed back into reality noticing it was only them. "You haven't touched your lunch. Are you feeling unwell?"

Heat crawled from Matilda's lower back to her neck, and sipped her cold tea. "No, I'm not sick. Sorry, my mind was distracted. I'll finish my lunch quickly."

"Yes, please do," said Miss Thames, peering at Matilda curiously and silence fell between them. "Matilda," she continued. "I must warn you to be cautious when it comes to matters of the heart."

If Matilda's heart beat any faster, it would explode from her chest.

"What do you mean?"

"I've seen it many times, and although Mr Fawlson carries

the swagger of a gentleman, you should be wary. Don't get me wrong, I think he is an amiable character, but he's young. It's not unknown that certain men love a challenge, particularly with a pretty young maid."

"Are you saying he's untrustworthy?"

She shook her head and offered a smile. "I don't want to see you hurt. Finish up your meal. You're going to need your strength on your way to visit your father."

"Thank you, Miss Thames," said Matilda, who gobbled up her lunch and accepted a warm cup of tea.

∽

GRINNING AT HER FATHER, Matilda played with her earlobe as she told him about Benedict. Her father leaned forward, eating up her every word.

"I'd love to meet him," Harold said with a soft nod and returned her smile.

"Miss Thames says I should be careful," Matilda said. Her voice dropped and her hands rested on her lap. "She thinks I might get hurt, but she thinks he's an honest gentleman."

Matilda shivered as she raised her eyes and glanced at her father. He'd lived at the prison for some time and she guessed he had become accustomed to the cold.

"Matilda, I'm sure she has your best interest at heart. You should listen to her, but you have the same look in your eyes as when I first met your mother."

Her head lifted and she noticed a comforting and proud expression on his face. Did he approve?

"When you first met Mam?"

"When I first saw her, I thought I'd stepped right into heaven. I didn't believe I'd met an angel," a faraway look filled his eyes and his face was covered in pure joy. "She stepped off the carriage, a wealthy family at that, and they didn't approve of me." His shoulders twitched into a shrug. "Not that I could blame them, I was in the wrong social class, but she stared at me as if I were the only man on earth."

Tears pricked the back of Matilda's eyes, her heart clenching as her father shared his true love moment he had had with her mother. But, as he spoke, she felt the same about Benedict. When she was around him, he made her smile, forget her worries and captivated her beyond words. It was as her father said, but it was Benedict that made her feel she was the only woman in the world.

Shock filled her from head to toe. Could it be possible that she held affection towards Benedict? Was this love she experienced whenever she was with him? His mischievous, charming smile—who knew an aristocrat's son had a quirky sense of humour—and she guessed if his father found out about his spontaneous actions, Benedict most likely would be disinherited or forbidden to see her. The idea of never seeing him again was agonising.

The guard slammed his stick against the bars as one would run a stick along a wooden fence. Her father's face glowered and he folded his arms over his chest. She understood his thoughts. Their time together was too little. Visiting him once a month was not enough.

"Trust your instinct," he offered a smile, but there were no creases at the corners of his eyes. "Time for exercise in the yard," he sighed and pushed his chair back.

Her heart sank watching him scuffle back inside the prison under the guard's supervision.

11
CONSCIOUS JUDGEMENT

A wavering high-pitched voice echoed from Miss Joan's room as Matilda walked past on her way to clean the guest room. Despite the Burlingtons' not entertaining guests, the room was expected to be cleaned. From the guest room, she heard Miss Joan's wails and chuckled. Whenever the governess taught math, the household heard Miss Joan's protests.

While she cleaned the guest room, Matilda continually glanced over her shoulder expecting Benedict's presence, but he did not come. Dejected, she thought over what Miss Thames said and realised perhaps what she said applied to Benedict. His absence indicated he was tired of her and she had to accept it.

Walking down the staircase, she overheard voices and her heart lifted; only for a second. She recognised Benedict's voice, but what if she'd offended him in some way? Would he confront her or ignore her?

Her feet touched the last stair and he turned to face her with a grim expression. Upon seeing her, his face lit up like the stars at night. She lowered her head, suppressing her smile, and greeted the gentlemen as she headed toward the drawing room.

She began dusting and wiping the tables when footsteps entered the drawing room. Expecting his charming smile, his face was downcast.

"Is everything all right, Mr. Fawlson?"

He gave a brief shake of his head. "I can't stay long. My father and I are late for an appointment, but I couldn't leave without seeing you."

Giddy, she stuck her hand inside her pocket. If anything would cheer him, surely he'd be thrilled to get his handkerchief back. She'd forgotten about it until she dug inside her suitcase searching for the one she'd made for her father.

Stretching her hand out to him, she beamed. "Here, I've kept this for you. Do you remember outside the court? It was you who gave me the handkerchief and it's beautiful. I can't keep it..." her voice trailed and she frowned staring at him.

"You...still...have...it?" he gulped, his face ashen. His breathing became ragged and heavy.

"Yes, of course, it's silk with your initials. Mr Fawlson, are you certain you're all right? Do I need to call the doctor?"

"No," he said with a weak smile and his eyes were filled with terror. "I...I..." he stammered, "I have plenty more, please keep it. I want you to keep it." He looked away and she noticed the feverish moisture that spread over his face and thought he looked ill.

"Oh?" Matilda pulled her hand back. "If there's anything wrong, please tell me."

The corners of his mouth twitched, but he couldn't offer a smile. Covering his face, he turned away and said, "I must go. My father's waiting for me."

Before Matilda could utter a word, he disappeared faster

than Miss Joan attempting to avoid math. Although his reaction was confusing, she presumed his work was busier than anticipated. Disappointment filled her heart. She would have liked to have offered him tea; like always, but at some point everyone has to complete their tasks no matter how tedious.

The drawing room had already been cleaned that morning and after wiping the tables and surfaces, she left making her way toward the laundry room. As she was about to turn, left of the staircase, she heard a scuffling noise from the master's study, located near the staircase. Curiosity overwhelmed her and swift on her feet, she crept closer to the study. Hadn't the meeting ended and everyone had left?

Peeking through the crack in the door, she covered her mouth as she gasped. What was Miss Joan doing in her father's study? The master made it clear no one was to enter except at the appointed cleaning schedule time. Miss Joan opened and closed drawer after drawer and she opened what appeared to be the last drawer and her mouth curled into a smile.

Matilda's brows raised staring at Miss Joan wide-eyed as she swiftly pulled bunches of crisp paper out of the drawer stuffing them inside her bodice. Glancing around there was no one around. Miss Joan appeared proud with a smile of satisfaction. She slammed the drawer shut and ran for the door. Matilda's heart thudded in her ribcage and she hid within the small cavity between the staircase and the study until she could no longer hear the young girl's footsteps.

Why would Miss Joan steal from her father? She was his pride and joy and he never denied her anything. Matilda's lips tightened as she snuck from beneath the staircase. It didn't make sense. Should she tell Miss Thames? No, she didn't think even Miss Thames would believe it. The mere idea of Miss Joan taking money from her father's study would sound ludicrous. A knot formed in her stomach as she made her way to the laundry, unable to push the thought from her mind.

∽

Lying in bed and listening to the serene quiet of the house, frogs croaked and insects trilled. Matilda's feelings played in her mind. First Benedict's strange behaviour, but she figured he had worries to tend to, but Miss Joan's actions proved otherwise. Should she tell someone? Abby and Mrs. McElfroy were always busy in the kitchen and she doubted their advice would help. If anyone it would be Miss Thames, but she'd tell Matilda to stay out of it. Pretend she saw nothing.

"Oh my..." Matilda whispered, clasping her hands to her chest. "What should I do? Everything seems like a bad idea, but how can I leave this alone? Lord, please send me guidance and the wisdom to handle this problem..." She paused and turned her head to listen. It was faint, but did someone call her name?

Sitting up she listened again. There was a sound and it was coming from outside the Burlingtons house. A cold shiver ran up her spine. That voice. It was Benedict, she was sure of it. Jumping out of bed, she stared out the window and exhaled a short breath in surprise. What was he doing here? He sounded drunk.

She put on her shoes and grabbed her coat, hoping no one had heard him. He wailed like the ferral cats in Whitechapel.

Rubbing her shoulders, she hurried down the staircase as fast as she could and down the hallway, careful not to slip; and unlocked the door.

"Benedict!" Matilda whispered in a hoarse voice. "Shush, keep your voice down you're going to wake the neighbourhood."

"I...yes...I..." he drawled, barely able to stand. She flushed at the sight of him. His trousers hung at his knees, his shirt dishevelled with no signs of his bow tie and one arm had slipped from his coat, flailing in the air.

He stared at her in desperation. His face was gaunt, his cheeks were tear-stained and his eyes were wild.

"I'm sorry...you...belie...me," he sprawled forward almost collapsing onto her, but he maintained his balance and slipped onto the stairs. "I...It's...fault..." he bawled, tears streaming down his face.

"I don't understand you, Benedict. Calm down," Matilda said, her eyes narrowing into a frown. "You don't make sense." She placed the other end of his coat over his shoulder, and ordered, "Stay quiet, I'm going to get you a glass of water."

His hand reached out and clutched her nightgown. "Don't...please," he slurred, "go, don't...please..." he hiccupped.

She pushed his hand away. "I'll be back, I promise."

He leant forward into a ball, hugging his legs, bowing his head and rocking back and forth.

"I'm sorry..." she heard him say as she bounded towards the kitchen.

Within minutes, she returned with a glass of water. "Drink this, you'll feel better." She recalled the countless nights she had to deal with her drunken father arriving home at awkward hours. What on earth could have caused Benedict to fall into such a state?

"What's happened?" she said.

Taking the glass of water from her, Benedict said, "Forgive me...Thank you, please...I...didn't..." he gulped the water.

"Forgive you for what?"

"What's going on here?" Miss Thames said, her voice full of irritation that rang in Matilda's ears.

Matilda stared at her as Benedict kept calling her name.

With a deep sigh, Miss Thames said, "All right, both of you, inside. Mr Fawlson, hush now."

Slurping the glass of water, Benedict slipped as he tried to stand and Matilda grasped the glass before he let it go. Placing it onto the top of the stair, she made a mental note to later collect the glass before it caught the Burlington's attention.

"What is he mumbling about?" Miss Thames heaved, as did Matilda, helping him walk up the stairs. "He can't stay in the guest room, we need to settle him in the vacant servant's room."

Matilda nodded, unable to breathe under his weight. She was reminded when Grover pushed her against the wall and shook the thought from her mind. This was different. Benedict needed their help.

Once Benedict was settled beneath the blankets in the servants' quarters, snoring away, Miss Thames led Matilda towards the kitchen.

"It's not like Mr Fawlson to behave this way. Are you sure you have no idea why he continued to call your name?"

Matilda shook her head, her fingers fanning over her eyes. "I don't know what he's talking about. Something about forgiveness and not his fault. I don't understand."

Miss Thames remained quiet but stood to her feet walked toward a cupboard and dug inside one of them. Pleased, she held up a half-full bottle of whiskey and placed it on the table.

"Whiskey?" she chuckled at the astonishment on Matilda's face. "For times such as this and I enjoy it now and then."

"No, thank you. I'll pass. I've seen too much of it and my mind is hazy."

"Suit yourself," Miss Thames said with a smile and lifted her glass in a salute, before taking a cavernous gulp. She poured herself another.

"Miss Thames, can I ask you something? I need advice."

"Yes, go ahead. If I have the answer I can help you." Her speech had slowed.

"If someone was known to have moral character and they prove otherwise, what should I do?"

"Hmm," Miss Thames rubbed her chin. "Well, people make mistakes all the time. I'm sure you know that more than anyone—"

"Yes," Matilda said, her head bobbing.

"—and the best thing to do is forgive them. Whatever the circumstances, it may be one that the person may not know how to handle it. If Mr Fawlson is calling out to you it means he trusts you. There must be a simple way this can be sorted out in the morning without his father or Mr Burlington discovering him here."

"Yes, you may be right," Matilda said, and she glanced at the table. Miss Thames was under the impression Matilda referred to Benedict. But, how could she explain it was Miss Joan on her mind?

"Do you know what it says in Luke six, verse thirty-seven?" Miss Thames said, swirling the last of the whiskey in her glass.

Matilda gaped at her in surprise. She never would've thought Miss Thames knew biblical scripture.

"It says, 'Judge not, and ye shall not be judged: condemn not, and ye shall not be condemned: forgive, and ye shall be forgiven.' Does this put your mind at rest?"

"I don't know," Matilda said.

"Don't worry, whatever the problem, it will sort itself out. Justice will eventually prevail and I know you believe in the Lord. Trust Him and know that He's in control all the time. Not in our time, but in His time."

"I appreciate your advice," Matilda said with a comforting smile. "I'll turn in for the night. I'm sure Bene—Mr Fawlson has an explanation for his behaviour tonight." She realised Miss Thames was right.

"Yes, we must keep this to ourselves, goodnight, Matilda."

With an unconvinced smile, Matilda returned the night-time farewell and rushed to collect the glass still near the stairs. Maybe she was overthinking it and what she thought she saw Miss Joan doing, may not be the correct impression. She decided to speak to Miss Joan in the morning and ask her about it.

Matilda headed upstairs and climbed back into bed slithering beneath her warm blankets and fell fast asleep.

12
UNEXPECTED REALITY

Making sure her uniform was neat and her hair braided into a bun making it easier to tuck within the pinned hairnet, Matilda added her white pinafore. She hoped Benedict was feeling better in the servant's quarters. It must be a shock for him to wake up in an unfamiliar place.

Her thoughts drifted to Miss Joan and she hesitated. Doubt filled her mind whether she should speak to Miss Joan or not. There was no way of knowing how much money she'd taken from her father's drawer, however, from Matilda's vantage point, it appeared to be a considerable amount.

She strode down the staircase making her way to the living room holding cleaning materials to dust and clean the carpet. Standing near the window, Matilda's heart tugged with pain recalling the last time her parents had been together. They stood in the garden of their house holding hands before her father left for work.

Light footsteps caught Matilda's attention and she observed Miss Joan yawn as she entered the room. Her brows pulled together and her nose wrinkled.

"Why are you here? Shouldn't you be elsewhere?" she said with a coy smile.

"Good day, Miss Joan, it's the scheduled time to clean the living room."

"It didn't look that way to me," she scoffed, elevating her chin. "You were staring out the window, no wonder the living room isn't cleaned properly."

Holding her tongue, Matilda blinked and said, "Miss Joan, yesterday I saw you leave the master's study in a hurry. What were you doing? Forgive my forwardness, but are you in trouble and need of money? I'm sure your father would assist if you talk to him."

Miss Joan's eyes widened with the whites showing and she took a step back. Her hands crossed over her chest. As she glanced away, Matilda noticed her chin trembling and her cheeks flushed.

"What do you know?" she said, her forehead puckering, and turning on her heels she bolted out of the living room.

Matilda stared after her open-mouthed and swallowed hard. What happened? She thought over her conversation with Miss Thames and was convinced Miss Joan was guilty of something. Miss Joan didn't offer an explanation or even deny taking the money. It was obvious that she stole money from her father, but why would she do that?

She shrugged and decided to let it go. If anything was amiss, she was certain Mr Burlington would have the matter resolved for his daughter.

Thumping, heavy pounding and scuffling resounded throughout the house. Matilda stopped sweeping the carpet and gazed at Mr Burlington's red face with Mr Penn and Miss Thames running after him.

"Get the servants now! I want everybody here this instant," his deep voice was wobbly and his frown deepened when he glimpsed at Matilda. A vein pulsated in his neck stroking his lengthy well-formed beard.

"Yes, Master Burlington, right away," said Mr Penn and Miss Thames simultaneously.

Tapping one of his polished black shoes, he demanded, "What's taking them so long?"

Miss Joan stood behind him with her body meandering toward the doorway averting her eyes from Matilda, who cocked a brow.

This immediate gathering can't have anything to do with the money, Matilda thought, her eyes darting at Miss Joan chewing her lip.

The floor rattled as a crowd of men and women entered the room all panic-stricken. All eyes darted around the living room, to Matilda, Miss Thames, at each other and Mr Burlington.

"Is this everyone?"

Mr Penn and Miss Thames bobbed their heads.

Miss Joan's eyes bore into Matilda and her lips curled into a mocking smile. A sense of dread rushed through Matilda's body and without doubt, she knew what this was all about. She cringed at the silence that followed.

Shifting of footsteps sliding across the floor caught the attention of everyone and Mr Burlingon's face crawled with confusion at the dishevelled appearance of Benedict. His hair was unkempt, his shirt unbuttoned, and dark rings beneath his eyes. Matilda was relieved that at least he had his trousers on properly.

"My head is pounding," he groaned, massaging his temples.

Miss Thames's eyes widened and shared a look of dismay with Matilda, who offered a reassuring smile from across the room.

"Mr Fawlson..." Mr Burlington stammered and blinked a few times in disbelief, but returned to the group before him. "I believe we have a thief in our midst."

The room was filled with gasps and murmurs of scepticism.

"Somehow, somebody knew I keep a certain lump sum of money inside one of the desk drawers in my study." His eyes peered at every person in the room. "I want the culprit to come forward and I might not press charges, however, your employment here will be discontinued."

When no one said a word, Mr Burlington stamped his foot against the floor. "Out with it, my patience is running thin. I'll fire all of you."

As Matilda was about to open her mouth, Miss Joan pointed in her direction. "Daddy, it's her. I'm sure of it. She cleaned your office. I walked right past and saw her inside your study."

"Hold on now," Benedict stepped forward and was completely sober. "Matilda would never do such a criminal act."

"Dare you to say I'm lying, Mr Fawlson?" Miss Joan challenged, her hands balled at her sides.

Glaring at her with anger, he said, "I don't believe it. It's someone else. Matilda would never. How many precious items do you possess in your home? Wouldn't she have taken something of extraordinary value?"

"I shall forget your words, Mr Fawlson," said Mr Burlington in a modulated tone, though rage overcame him. "How you came to be in this state at my home I dread for an answer. For the sake of your family and business, I shall forget you were here. This is a private matter and I suggest you leave."

"Look in her room, Daddy," Joan said, her cheeks flushed as

she held onto her father's arm. "If she took it the only place would obviously be inside her nightstand or her bed."

Matilda stared at her dumbstruck. For Miss Joan to be dauntingly specific it was obvious the money would be found somewhere in her area. It never occurred to her that Miss Joan could stoop to a level this low.

"Mr Penn, please stay here and ensure no one leaves this room." Mr Burlington leered at Matilda and pointed at her. "Particularly that one." His eyes landed on Miss Thames. "Come and show me her quarters."

Miss Thames side-glanced at Matilda with a sad smile as if she knew the money would be found. Matilda closed her eyes and drew in a deep breath to keep her body from shaking. She couldn't lose her employment and she knew no one, except for the staff would believe her. If she ran away it would imply her being guilty.

Thudding and angry ranting bellowed through the house. Mr Burlington puffed as though he'd run a marathon, his face if at all possible, had darkened to crimson. He scowled at her, scrunching up a bunch of money in his thick hands. Miss Thames's eyes were moist and kept her head low.

"I told you, Daddy," she smirked at Mr Fawlson. "See, I wasn't lying."

"Everyone back to work," Mr Burlington raged, his eyes bulging with anger. "I gave you a chance, lodging, and meals, and at Miss Thames' recommendation promoted you from the kitchen."

Matilda remained silent and felt Benedict's eyes on her. Even if she spoke up and tried to explain. it was Miss Joan, the money had been found somewhere in the room she shared with three other maids. How did Miss Joan guess where she slept? Either she threatened one of the other maids or planted the money somewhere convincing it was found in Matilda's area.

"Don't go anywhere," Mr Burlington ordered and walked out of the room demanding his carriage to be ready.

"Matilda," said Benedict hurrying to her side. He placed his hands over her shoulders and he searched her face. "I believe you, I know you didn't steal that money."

"It was Miss Joan who took the money," Matilda said, hoping she could trust him with this information. "She's set me up because I caught her."

His head tilted back and he gaped at her in horror. "Why didn't you say anything?"

Her eyes glistened as she swallowed the intense emotions threatening to explode. "Who would believe a maid's word against the daughter of a wealthy businessman?"

"You're right. I'm sorry, Matilda, I know you didn't do this," he said removing his hands. Benedict's eyes lay on the table and guilt coated his face. "But no one will believe you."

Mr Penn returned to the living room. His eyes were hazy, staring at Matilda as if her fate was worse than death, and through gritted teeth, "Be careful, Matilda, none of us believe it. I-I've come to take you to the carriage."

"Take me, too," said Mr Fawlson catching Mr Penn off-guard, who nodded with his mouth half-open. "I'll go fighting if I have to."

"No need, Mr Fawlson. There's plenty of space in the carriage," Mr Penn, his shoulders slumped and gestured for them to follow him.

Mr Penn closed the carriage door and held up a handkerchief to his eyes. Matilda placed her hand on the window and gave him a brave smile. She would have liked to have spoken to Malcolm, who had made a full recovery, but the master forbade anyone to speak with her.

The sound of grinding wheels escalated her throbbing heart. Would she ever see her father again?

Benedict said in a husky voice, "I'm sure if you tell the judge what happened, they'll let you free."

Matilda swiped her eyes with her forefinger. "I don't know about that," she sniffled, "my father was falsely accused and it's clear the judges and jury were paid off. He should have been set free, there was not enough evidence."

"You're worried about your father," he stared at her with flared nostrils. "You're future is at stake and all you're concerned about is your father?"

Angling her body towards him, she tilted her neck, and said, "I'm sorry, Benedict. I doubt you've faced anything such as this and don't expect you to understand. My father may think I've deserted him."

He opened his mouth, it snapped shut. Sitting upright, he placed his hand on the seat wriggling his hand until his pinky finger touched hers. She swallowed, it felt warm, and lifted her head locking eyes with him.

"It's going to be all right," he said, eyes brightening with a warm smile. "I'll be with you every step of the way."

13
UNEXPECTED TRUTH

Furiously rubbing her arms, Matilda huddled on the tiny steel cot with a thin mattress and a shredded piece of material for a blanket. How had her father survived in prison? The stone walls and floors accentuated the cold cell, which was the size of a scullery kitchen. There was another woman in prison, who remained silent and was not eager to converse. The only response was cussing and swearing in words she'd never heard of before.

"You'll have to lock me behind the bars to keep me away."

It was Benedict's voice and his fury reached her ears. Did he plan on staying with her? If he didn't back down, he'd certainly be arrested and spend the night in prison.

"Sir, you need to leave. It's against the rules—"

"I am the son of a diplomat. One message and you'll be without a job," Benedict threatened to Matilda's horror. If only her voice could reach past the cells, she'd tell him to go home.

Banging and clashing mixed with resentful groans followed the clanging of keys unlocking squeaking gates and footsteps clopped on the stones until they stopped at her cell.

She lifted her chin, lips dry and teeth chattering, and disgust fell upon his face. "Gracious men, can't you provide a decent blanket? She'll get a chill of a cold."

"Hey, this isn't the fancy hotel you've been to," the police officer chirped, but one dark look from Benedict sent the guard on his heels in search of a warm blanket.

"What about you?" Matilda said thanking the police officer for the warm blanket.

Squaring his shoulders and flashing his dashing lop-sided grin, he said, "I'll be fine. Thanks to you, I have my coat." He pulled his hat over his forehead. "Get some rest, Matilda, tomorrow will be a wearisome day for you."

Matilda dragged the blanket over her shoulders to her chin and gazed at Benedict sleeping on the wooden bench. He removed his waistcoat for a pillow and covered his upper body with his coat. No matter how hard she tried, she couldn't sleep. The events played in her mind. How could Miss Joan betray her and lie about it? She'd always been polite to the young girl and tried her utmost to assist where she could.

The more her mind plagued over everything, the words of scripture Miss Thames had shared with her removed all doubt. The deep void in her heart was filled with comfort and strength. Glancing at Benedict, she appreciated his bravery in standing up for her and realised she loved him.

Before long, her eyes fluttered and darkness fell around her.

∼

MATILDA WAS NOT unfamiliar with the rules of the police station. The annoying clanking of the baton against the bars woke her and her cell mate. The other woman responded as if she'd learnt the English dialect from a sailor.

"Wake up, cupid," the guard mocked the other woman with a light smirk. He opened his mouth, gazing at Matilda, but thought better of it when he noticed Benedict's dark piercing expression. "Yeah," he surveyed the area before disappearing.

A man dressed in black walked in through the door that led to the backrooms and the kitchen. He tossed a tin bowl with white slop inside and the same for the other woman. He eyed Benedict and stared down at him with a disdainful look, and huffed, "Don't get ideas, you are not getting any."

Benedict's shoulder shook and he chuckled. Matilda enjoyed his playful laugh.

"I pity anyone who'd want to eat that."

They laughed and for whatever reason, tears of laughter slid down her cheeks, but only for a brief moment she felt joy.

The sound of heavy boots ricocheted around the cells. Two bobbies marched in unison toward Matilda's cell. She thought of the inspector, who'd interviewed her before. Was anyone going to interview her now?

She held out her arms and one of the bobbies cuffed her wrists and spun her around. Nudging her forward, Matilda walked with them past the front desk counter and out of the station. Benedict was close behind her.

Matilda grimaced at the sound of rattling, clanking and what sounded like an iron ball scraped against the floor. She was relieved to leave the police station but knew the prison was worse. The idea of not visiting her father alarmed her.

Despite the carriage being one to only transport prisoners, bobbies had realised it was pointless to argue with Benedict and permitted him to join Matilda. She shuddered at the sight of the same courthouse where her father had been convicted.

"Like father, like daughter," she heard one of the guards snicker as she climbed out of the carriage. She blinked back tears and bit her lip to suppress her whirlwind of emotions. Of course, they'd remember her.

Benedict shot them a chilling glare and the guards pressed their lips and turned their faces away, eyes darting everywhere but at Matilda.

She was led to the the same court room and the guard uncuffed her at the dock without a chair. Her heart pounded and she glanced at Benedict seated at the stall allocated for family and friends. His face was full of anger and irritation, but when he turned towards her, he gave her a thumbs-up with a reassuring smile.

Everything was the same, except there was no jury, only one judge, and the prosecutor, Mr Charles Hatton. He appeared as though he'd just graduated from law school. He stood at his desk with the solicitor behind him. Mr Burlington insisted he stay with the prosecutor. Thankfully, Benedict had managed to call George to represent her. They all wore white wigs, but the wig upon the Judge's head had an elaborate design.

Miss Joan sat two spaces away from Benedict and Matilda hoped the girl would come to her senses. Remembering what happened to her father, Matilda's heart streaked with pain. It would become her fate, too.

The judge tapped his gavel upon his podium and everyone became silent. The clerk held a folder and elevating his pasty face, declared the charges Matilda had been accused of. Drawing in deep breaths, she had to remain calm no matter what anyone said.

"The defendant, Miss Matilda Wenslow, has been charged with the heinous crime of thievery by the complainant Mr Oscar Burlington."

Matilda gulped and her body chilled, but not from the icy wind that escaped inside the room, which was as suffocating as she remembered it to be. Her ears pricked at the sound of Mr Hatton's shrilly, singsong voice.

"Your Honour as the prosecuting solicitor, Charles Hatton, I shall prove beyond all doubt that the defendant is guilty of the crime of thievery."

The ridiculous notion pounded in Matilda's head. This can't be happening. If she closed her eyes and reopened them it would be a dream, but she heard the clerk's voice and opened her eyes.

"Miss Wenslow, how do you plead?"

Her hands were clammy and her clothes tightened, she opened her mouth, but no sound came out.

"Miss Wenslow, how do you plead? I shall not ask again unless your silence is an admission of guilt."

"Not guilty," she said in a soft voice, lower lip quivering. How had her father declared his innocence with such passion, yet all she could do was whimper? She had to be strong and fight, she was innocent. She stole a glance at Miss Joan, who nibbled on her lip set in a tight line.

"Guilty!" Mr Burlington bellowed, which started yelling and cheers from the public crowd and whomever he'd invited.

The judge pounded his gavel and screamed for order.

Once the room fell silent, Matilda decided this was her chance and prayed the judge would allow her to speak.

A spark of adrenaline rushed through her veins and a strength she'd never felt before struck her like a bolt of lightning.

"Your Honour," she spoke with a voice of confidence, ignoring George's raised eyebrows and the faces fixed onto her with horror. "If you will, I'd like to say something. I understand this does not fall part of the court's rules, but please hear my humble request."

The court exploded with anger urged by Mr Burlington and again the judge tapped his gavel ordering silence.

"Mr Burlington," the judge's voice rose with irritation. "One more word from you and I'll hold you in contempt of court."

His face paled and with a brief nod, he stared at his jutting stomach.

The judge's face perked with interest and Matilda wondered if she should thank Mr Burlington for his unruly outburst.

The clerk and the prosecutor's jaws dropped when the judge said, "Yes, Miss Wenslow. I'm curious to hear what you have to say."

"Thank you, Your Honour," Matilda bobbed her head. "I will not cast blame and have no ill feelings to those who deem me guilty and," she blew out a deep breath, "I hold no grudge against anyone and understand the ways of this world. Innocent or guilty it favours those who live in wealth without pity to those who ache through pain and hardship. Whatever you decide, I will honour the punishment that may be imparted to me."

The judge leaned back folding his arms and his brows knitted. From where she stood, Matilda could not tell what he may be thinking.

"Stop, stop!" a young woman wailed from the bench. "It was me, I did it. Miss Wenslow did not take the money, I did."

The court erupted and Mr Burlington glared at his daughter gobsmacked. His face turned red, and his jaw tensed as he lifted his hands curled into fists against his chest.

"You don't know what you're saying, Joan. You must be sick with worry," Mr Burlington insisted, his deep voice cracked.

The judge slammed his gavel screaming for order and the room fell silent.

"Is this true?" the judge demanded, leaning forward. Matilda noticed the anger on his face.

Miss Joan nodded and bawled, covering her face with her hands. "I'm sorry, I am. Matilda, I'm sorry, what I did was wrong."

"Mr Burlington, seeing as your daughter has confessed do you wish to press charges?" the judge glowered at the man, who pulled his shoulders back, pupils dilated.

"No, Your Honour," he said. His deep voice was heightened by two octaves. "I will handle this matter on my own."

"Miss Wenslow," the judge said with a tug at his lips. "You're free to go." And he slammed the gavel firmly.

"I can't bear this anymore," Benedict shouted and stood, clutching the wooden railing. "I'm guilty."

"What now?" the judge said, irritation coating his crimson face. "This is not a play ground, this is a place of justice! The crime was thievery and the defendant has been found not guilty."

The immense joy that overwhelmed Matilda now turned into confusion staring at Benedict. What was going on? First Miss Joan confessed it was her, but what was Benedict on about?

"Matilda, I'm sorry, it was an accident. I swear it was." Benedict's words grew faster and his face scrunched up. "Your father didn't kill that man..." he choked on his words, heaving, "The man was harassing the bar lady and I only wanted to help her. I forced him outside, he was drunk and began throwing fists at me. I'm not a fighter and all I did was push him. He lost his balance and fell down the stairs."

"Quiet," the judge slammed his gavel, but Benedict ignored him.

"I love you, Matilda, I cannot lie. Every time I look at you, I'm reminded of what I've done. My father covered it up." He stared at the judge with tears streaming down his face. "Your Honour, please take me away. Free Harold Wenslow. I can't bear the guilt anymore. It's tearing me apart."

"Is this your confession to the murder of Mr Andrew Henslop?"

"Yes, Your Honour. I will place my hand over the Bible. I swear it. It was my fault the man died and without my consent my father covered it up, blaming Math—Miss Wenslow's father."

"Very well," the judge said and commanded, "Bailiff take this man…"

"Mr Benedict Fawlson," he introduced himself.

"Take Mr Fawlson into custody."

"I don't expect you to forgive me," Benedict hurried down the stairs and raced to Matilda. "My love for you is real. Will you wait for me—"

"Come on, pretty boy," a guard clamped thick arms over Benedict's shoulder pulling him away.

"—Please, I want to prove myself. I'll pay the price—"

"Quiet, before I shut that mouth for you," the guard growled.

"Yes, Benedict," said Matilda, her chest expanding as her breath came out in gasps. "I forgive you, I understand. I'll wait for you."

She stretched her neck and a warm sensation tugged at her heart as he gave her one last lop-sided grin before being dragged below the courthouse and into the cell.

14
A HAPPY REUNION

Matilda clasped her hands with excitement. Waiting was the worst. What was taking so long?

Finally, the Newgate Prison gates roared open. Her heart soared with the birds above the clouds as she gazed at the familiar hearty smile that reached his ears and his eyes were moist. He was dressed in brown pants, a white shirt with a drawstring at his neck and black scruffy boots.

"Papa," yelled Matilda dashing towards her father and embracing him like never before, enjoying his firm arms around her. "I can't believe this is happening. Justice does happen."

"I don't want to let go," Harold whispered into her ear. "It may be a dream. One I have had every night."

"It's real, Papa," Matilda grinned and glimpsed at Mr Burlington standing near his carriage waving his forefinger at an embarrassed Miss Joan. "Though I fear I don't have a place to call home."

"You're my home," he said, pulling away and staring into her eyes. "As long as we're together, that's home."

"You're stronger, Papa. What work did they make you do?"

"I'm not going to tell you, but I am going to say that I desire roast beef, potatoes and pudding." His shoulders shook with laughter and he stroked her cheek. "It was hard at first, but I got over alcohol and will never drink it again."

"That's wonderful, Papa, I'm proud of you. Mam would be proud, too."

He grabbed her shoulders and hugged her again. "I'll be a better father and I promise I'll never let you down again."

Overcome with happiness at the release of her father, Matilda couldn't help but think about Benedict and how he'd face the same conditions as her father.

As if reading her mind, Harold said with a sympathetic look in his eyes, "I heard about Benedict. I'm sorry, I know you care a lot about him. It takes courage and strength for someone to admit their guilt, especially one for murder. He's a diplomat's son so I imagine he won't have it as bad. Don't worry, he'll be fine and out in two years."

"What do you think Mr Fawlson will do?"

"He'll have nothing to do with my business, that's what!" boomed Mr Burlington's voice, taking Matilda and her father by surprise. They hadn't heard him approach. His jaw tensed as he lifted his chin and stared at them. "He'll be busy cleaning up the scandalous disaster he created. I doubt anyone will have dealings with him again."

Mr Burlington's silk top hat was tight on top of his head as he turned towards Matilda with a glassy look in his eyes. "I'm sorry. My daughter will be punished for her actions," he shook his head with shame, "I don't know how to make it up to you, except to offer your old job back. That is if you would like it."

Matilda and her father exchanged a beaming smile. "Yes, of course, I want my job back."

He cleared his throat. "Now that I am without a business

partner I find myself in need of assistance for a construction supervisor. You see I'm in the business of property development and unfortunately, embarrassing to say, is that without Mr Fawlson's financial backing, work will be delayed." His sigh came out with great effort. "Mr Wenslow, I hear you have experience in construction, do you not?"

"Yes, sir, I do."

"I am deeply mortified at the actions of my daughter and cannot apologise enough. With my plight, I now require a construction supervisor and offer you the position if you are interested. There is a small house on my property where you can stay. Miss Wenslow may decide to stay with you or remain in the house. Please inform Miss Thames of your decision."

Mr Burlington offered his hand and Harold pumped it.

"So, are we in agreement?"

"Yes, sir. When should I start?"

"I'll give you a week to settle. I'm sure you'd like to enjoy freedom after being locked away in that dump for that extended period."

Matilda stifled a smile. Mr Burlington had no idea what it was like at the prison or what it was like to be a prisoner.

"We appreciate your kindness," Harold said, unable to stop smiling.

With a curt nod, Mr Burlington turned, running his hand over his black frock coat as if it were covered in dust and walked toward the carriage where Miss Joan was seated.

"You like working for the Burlington's don't you?"

"Yes, I've made many friends, but I had to sell all our belongings. Everything except for Mam's jewellery."

"It's all right," Harold wrapped his arm around Matilda's shoulders. "There's a house waiting for us. I'd like for you to stay with me."

"I'd love that," Matilda said without hesitation, and the

corners of her mouth quirked upward. "I wouldn't have it any other way."

His forehead puckered, fighting back tears, but he lost the battle and tears flowed down his cheeks. "I've dreamt of this day," he sniffled, "I'm sorry, it feels like a miracle. I prayed every night." He wiped his tears and nose with the back of his hand.

"Why don't we go see Miss Thames and I know Mrs McElfroy will cook the best you've ever eaten."

"Everything seems different," he said. His eyes perused the building and then the streets. Turning to her, he said, "No, I think nothing has changed."

Giggling, Matilda and her father walked down Whitechapel Street and he nodded as she chattered away to him about everything.

15
EPILOGUE

FIVE YEARS LATER

Hope and cheer billowed in the air, a gentle breeze weaving through Matilda's hair as she sat at the top of the hill at Kensington Park. She gazed at her two-year-old daughter, Adeline—after her mother—and Benedict playing near the edge of the lake. The colourful bushes rustled and the bulrushes and cattails caught in the wind moved as though waving at her.

Statues and fountains with water trickling into the lake had been erected in honour of Queen Victoria. Some were of cherubs holding up a large decorative dish with spurting lake water or of people holding a jar with liquid pouring out of it and into the lake. Trees scattered around the lake reflected like a mirror from the lake.

She loved working at the Burlington's house, groomed to become the next housekeeper under the supervision of Miss Thames. Because her father was the manager of Mr Burlington's construction, he was able to take on Benedict as his apprentice.

Matilda recalled how Mr Fawlson had disgraced his son when he'd served his time in prison and was released. She'd accompanied her husband to the house in Fulham Street and Mr Fawlson acted as though he did not have an elder son. Disinherited from the family's fortune, everything would fall to his younger brother, Edward. What Mr Fawlson didn't realise was that his sons had a close relationship.

She'd never seen such freedom on Benedict's face as he introduced Matilda as his loving wife to his father, who slammed the door in his face. It was unquestionable that her father and husband were two of the bravest and kindest men in the world.

Holding Adeline's tiny, dimpled hand, Benedict led her towards Matilda.

"Ma...ma...am," cooed Adeline reaching her hands out to her mother. With a proud grin, Matilda drew her daughter into a tight embrace and breathed in the scent of baby powder and cream.

"Should we leave, honey?" Benedict said, leaning over and placing his hand on her back. "How are you feeling?" he added, gazing with affection at her growing belly.

"Yes, let's go," Matilda stared up at him with love. She'd never believed that she'd find true happiness like her parents had, but here she was with the man of her dreams and a growing family. "My father and Miss Thames will arrive for lunch and I need to make pudding."

Taking Adeline into his arms, he helped her to her feet. "You work too hard, please don't overexert yourself. I'm sure Mrs McElfroy would help."

With a mischievous grin, she said, "Yes, she does bake the

most delicious chocolate cake, but I believe she's busy today. Mr Burlington is hosting a ball for Miss Joan's matrimony."

Benedict snorted a chuckle, "I'd pay to see her face. I can't imagine how excited she must be."

"Stop teasing," Matilda said, nudging her husband with a soft chortle. "Though, I'd love to see it, too. I'm sure Miss Thames will fill in the details."

Adeline groaned and shifted in Benedict's arms, niggling for her mother.

"She's hungry," said Matilda. "It's a good thing we brought the extra bottle."

Benedict placed her inside the stroller and gave her a glass bottle of milk. Adeline accepted the bottle without fuss and sucked at the teat.

Matilda hooked her arm over Benedict's arm, and he pushed the stroller towards their home only a few blocks away on High Kensington Street.

THE END

THE FIRST CHAPTER OF 'THE WORKHOUSE ORPHAN RIVALS'
BY RACHEL DOWNING

Charlotte Ripley giggled as she scampered down the cobblestone streets, her pigtails bouncing with each step. The warm summer sun cast a golden glow over the bustling city, and the air was thick with the aromas of fresh bread and chimney smoke.

"Wait for me!" called a voice from behind her.

Charlotte spun around, her hazel eyes sparkling, as Lucas

Alcott rounded the corner. His cheeks were flushed and he doubled over, panting.

"You're too fast, Charlie," he said, using the nickname that only he was allowed to call her.

Charlotte grinned, not the least bit apologetic. "You'll have to keep up then, won't you?"

Lucas straightened, a playful gleam in his eyes. "Oh, I'll keep up all right." With that, he took off after her, his feet pounding against the uneven stones.

A squeal of delight escaped Charlotte as she fled, weaving through the throngs of people going about their daily business. Vendors hawked their wares, horses whickered, and the general cacophony of the city surrounded them, but in that moment, it was just the two of them, lost in their childish game of chase.

Finally, Charlotte ducked into a narrow alleyway, pressing her back against the cool brick as Lucas skidded to a halt in front of her.

"I caught you," Lucas panted, leaning against the opposite wall.

"For now," Charlotte countered, her eyes twinkling. "But you'll never catch me for good."

Lucas smiled. "You'll never get rid of me, Charlie."

"Over here!" Lucas hissed, gesturing towards a small nook between two buildings. Charlotte followed him, her heart pounding with excitement at the prospect of a new discovery.

Tucked away in the shadows was an old wooden crate, its contents spilling out onto the ground. Lucas knelt down, sifting through the debris with eager hands.

"Look at this!" he exclaimed, holding up a tarnished pocket watch. Its face was cracked, but the intricate engravings along the side still caught the light.

Charlotte gasped, taking the watch gingerly in her hands.

"It's beautiful," she breathed, running her fingers over the delicate etchings.

Lucas grinned. "It's yours, then. It's definitely some great treasure. I'm sure it's got all sorts of mysterious hidden away in it. We'll just have to work them out."

Warmth blossomed in Charlotte as she clutched the watch to her heart. This was why she loved Lucas so dearly – he always knew how to make her feel special, like she was the most important person in his world.

Their adventures continued, each day a new escapade. One afternoon found them perched high in the branches of a gnarled oak tree, swapping stories and dreams as the leaves whispered secrets around them.

"When I'm grown," Lucas declared, "I'm going to sail the seas and see the whole world."

Charlotte wrinkled her nose. "The whole world? What about me?"

"Of course you'll come too," he said matter-of-factly. "We'll have grand adventures together, you and I. We'll never be apart."

Charlotte smiled, comforted by the promise in his words.

Then there were the days spent racing through the streets, their shouts of laughter carrying on the warm breeze. Tag was their favourite game, a whirlwind of darting bodies and breathless taunts.

These were the moments Charlotte cherished, the memories she knew she would hold dear for the rest of her life. In those carefree days of childhood, with Lucas by her side, she felt invincible, as though nothing could ever tarnish the innocence of their bond.

∼

Charlotte watched her parents with admiration as they prepared for their day's work. Even at her young age, she understood the sacrifices they made to provide a stable home for her.

Robert Ripley rose before the sun, his movements quiet yet purposeful as he dressed for the docks. Charlotte heard the creak of the wooden floors as he laced up his heavy boots. When he emerged from the bedroom, his face was etched with determination, a man ready to tackle another gruelling day of labor.

"Off to earn our bread, little one," he said, ruffling Charlotte's hair affectionately. Despite the early hour, his eyes crinkled with a warm smile.

Charlotte nodded solemnly. "Be safe, Papa."

With a final nod, Robert strode out the door. Charlotte knew the docks were an unforgiving place, the work arduous and unrelenting, but her father embraced it without complaint. He was a man of quiet strength, unwavering in his commitment to provide for his family.

As the front door closed behind Robert, Jane emerged from the kitchen, her hands already busy tying the strings of her apron. "Good morning, my darling," she said, pressing a kiss to Charlotte's forehead. "Did you sleep well?"

Charlotte nodded, though truthfully, she had been awake for some time, lying in bed and listening to the familiar sounds of her parents' morning routine. It was a comforting ritual, one that anchored her in a sense of security and love.

Jane headed back into the kitchen, bustled around packing her midwife's bag with the necessary tools and supplies. Her movements were efficient yet gentle, a testament to the care she brought to her work. Charlotte knew that her mother's calling was more than just a job – it was a sacred duty, one she embraced with all her heart.

"A new babe is coming into the world today," Jane said, her eyes shining with anticipation. "Isn't that a wondrous thing?"

Charlotte nodded again, her heart swelling with pride. Her mother was a beacon of strength and compassion, a guiding light for those in need.

As Jane gathered the last of her things, she paused to smooth Charlotte's unruly curls. "Mind the house for me, won't you, love? I'll be back before you know it."

With a final kiss and a whispered "I love you," Jane swept out the door, her steps purposeful and her head held high.

Charlotte watched her parents go, their paths diverging into the bustling streets of London, and felt a profound sense of gratitude. Though their work was humble, their dedication knew no bounds. It was through their unwavering efforts that Charlotte's world remained secure, a haven of love and stability in an ever-changing city.

∼

CHARLOTTE'S FEET carried her down the familiar path, her steps light and carefree as she made her way to Lucas's home. The warm summer breeze tousled her hair, and she couldn't help but skip a little, filled with the boundless energy of youth.

As she rounded the corner, the modest dwelling came into view – a humble abode, but one that radiated a sense of comfort and familiarity. Charlotte could already picture Lucas waiting for her, his face alight with that infectious grin that never failed to make her heart swell.

She rapped her knuckles against the weathered door, the sound echoing within the stillness of the narrow street. A gruff voice called out, bidding her entry, and Charlotte slipped inside.

The interior was simple but well-kept, a reflection of the

hardworking man who presided over the household. Charles Alcott sat hunched at the small dining table, his broad shoulders straining against the fabric of his shirt as he pored over a tattered ledger. Even in repose, his frame exuded a rugged strength, forged by years of toiling at the docks.

"Mornin', Miss Ripley," he greeted, his voice a deep rumble. He glanced up, and Charlotte was struck by the intensity of his gaze, those piercing blue eyes that mirrored Lucas's own.

"Good morning, Mr Alcott," she replied, dipping into a polite curtsy.

Charles waved a calloused hand, dismissing the formality. "None of that, now. You're like family 'round these parts." A ghost of a smile tugged at his mouth, softening the harsh lines of his weathered visage.

Charlotte lips curved upwards in response, her heart warmed by the gruff affection he so freely offered. Despite his rough exterior, there was an undeniable tenderness in the way Charles regarded her, a silent acknowledgment of the bond she shared with his son.

As if summoned by her thoughts, Lucas emerged from the back room, his face lighting up at the sight of her. "Charlie!"

Charles's expression shifted, his features melting into an unguarded display of love and pride as he watched his son approach. In that moment, Charlotte glimpsed the depths of his affection, a love so profound that it seemed to eclipse the lingering sorrow that clung to him like a shroud.

For she knew, beneath the gruff exterior and calloused hands, Charles Alcott carried a wound that had never truly healed – the loss of his beloved wife during the very act of bringing their son into the world. It was a pain that had shaped him, hardening his resolve to be both mother and father to the boy who was now his entire world.

And as Lucas threw his arms around his father in a fierce

embrace, Charlotte saw it all – the love, the grief, the unwavering devotion that bound this small family together. It was a poignant reminder that even in the humblest of circumstances, the human spirit would shine through, a beacon of resilience and hope in the face of adversity.

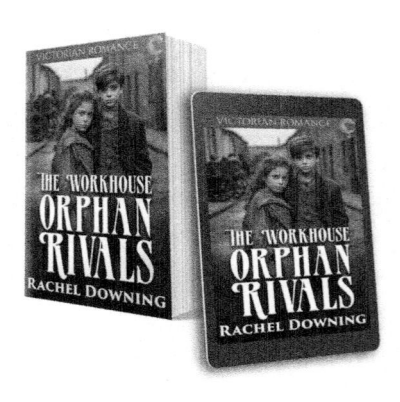

**Clear here to read the rest of
The Workhouse Orphan Rivals'**

Childhood sweethearts torn apart. A promise broken. A love that refuses to die.

In the gritty underbelly of Victorian London, Charlotte Ripley's dreams are shattered when her childhood love, Lucas Alcott, chooses ambition over their bond. Thrust into the very workhouses she once feared, Charlotte fights to survive—never expecting to see Lucas again.

But fate has other plans.

When Lucas reappears as her new foreman, old feelings reignite amidst a powder keg of resentment and desire. Can Charlotte forgive the boy who broke her heart? Or will the dashing footman Brandon Johnson sweep her off her feet in her new life as a maid?

As secrets unravel and danger lurks in the shadows, Charlotte must decide who to trust—and who truly deserves her heart.

From workhouse grime to aristocratic shine, this gripping tale of love, betrayal, and redemption will keep you turning pages long into the night. Watch as childhood promises collide with adult realities, testing the limits of forgiveness and the power of true love.

'The Workhouse Orphan Rivals'

OUR GIFT TO YOU

AS A WAY TO SAY THANK YOU WE WOULD LOVE TO SEND YOU THIS BEAUTIFUL STORY FREE OF CHARGE.

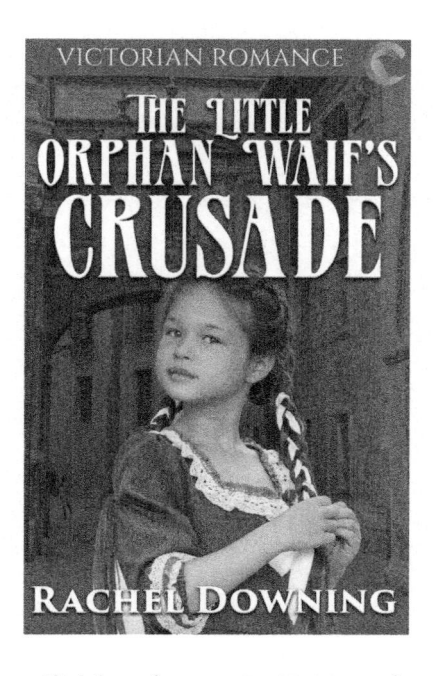

Click here for your FREE COPY of

'The Little Orphan Waif's Crusade'

CornerstoneTales.com/sign-up

In the wake of her father's passing, seven-year-old Matilda is determined to heal her sister Effie's shattered spirit.

Desperate to restore joy to Effie's life, Matilda embarks on a daring quest, aided by the gentle-hearted postman, Philip. Together, they weave a plan to ignite the flame of love in Effie's heart once more.

At Cornerstone Tales we publish books you can trust. Great tales without sex or swearing, but with all of the mystery and romance you expect from a great story.

Be the first to know when we release new books, take part in our fun competitions, and get surprise free books in your inbox by signing up to our free VIP Reader list.

As a thank you you'll receive a copy of 'The Little Orphan Waif's Crusade' by *Rachel Downing* straight away, alongside other gifts.

Click here to sign up for our mailing list, and receive your FREE stories.

CornerstoneTales.com/sign-up

LOVE VICTORIAN ROMANCE?

Books by our other Victorian Romance Writer *RACHEL DOWNING*

Two Steadfast Orphan's Dreams

Follow the stories of Isabella and Ada as they overcome all odds and find love.

Get 'Two Steadfast Orphan's Dreams' Here!

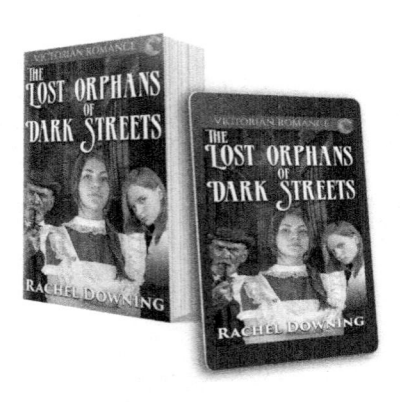

The Lost Orphans of Dark Streets

Follow the stories of Elizabeth and Molly as they negotiate the dangerous slums and find their place in the world.

Get 'The Lost Orphans of Dark Streets' Here!

The Orphan Prodigy's Stolen Tale

When ten-year-old Isabella Farmerson's world shatters with the tragic loss of her parents, she's thrust into a life of hardship and uncertainty.

Get 'The Orphan Prodigy's Stolen Tale' Here!

The Workhouse Orphan Rivals

Childhood sweethearts torn apart. A promise broken. A love that refuses to die.

Get 'The Workhouse Orphan Rivals' Here!

If you enjoyed this story, sign up to our mailing list to be the first to hear about our new releases and any sales and deals we have.

We also want to offer you a Victorian Romance novella - 'The Little Orphan Waif's Crusade' - absolutely free!

Click here to sign up for our mailing list, and receive your FREE stories.

CornerstoneTales.com/sign-up